Laia Kodorko stumbled through the streets of the town with her eyes wide open and her hands held before her. She stumbled forward, never blinking, her hands moving in flat arcs.

Her face wasn't remotely human; it was absolutely motionless, absolutely passionless. Something stared out of it at me. It wasn't anything I'd ever imagined before.

Nobody said anything for a moment. She stopped and just watched me—whatever she was.

I said: "Who are you?"

Her voice was flat and lifeless. "We are here. We have always been here. We cannot be resisted."

"What do you want?" I asked.

"We want every human on the planet to leave immediately, forever. All who stay will die."

That's when the fighting started.

Laurence M. Janifer (married; two children one each; the M. is for Mark) is 44 years old, calendar time. He is 5' 10'' high and weighs less than you would believe. His hair is brown and fairly short, and he has owned a small, neat moustache and beard (red-brown) for nearly twenty years now. He wears dark, severe suits with vests to them because he has always done so, and he wears horn-rimmed glasses both because he has always done so and because without them he would get very little reading done, and not much straight seeing either. Even with his glasses on, he has a tendency to bump into things. Nothing can be done about this.

He has written over 35 published books, and just under 500 magazine pieces, under a discouraging variety of names. Among all these are three collaborations with the late S.J. Treibich, for Ace. (He has also collaborated with Randall Garrett—as ''Mark Phillips''—and with a small handful of other authors.) He now writes only under his own name: nearly all the other names were used as characters in one of his books, which seems to have finished them.

He likes to read, watch movies (he was a movie reviewer for a while, and he calls them movies, not films), and play large swatches of jazz, classical or show-tune piano, and he is still trying to keep up with a scattering of mathematics, particle physics, rocketry, psychiatry and medicine, and politics. He believes, by faith, in the existence of a real world out there, but he spends a lot of time with the one inside his head.

Mr. Janifer drinks very little and smokes too much. He prefers Knave's cigarettes, but finds the brand hard to locate these days. He likes writing unnecessarily long letters, and he answers all the letters the Post Office is willing to give him. Between letters, he is writing some more books, of which a majority at the moment are sf. He has had nine poems published. His eyes are brown.

He argues a lot. He shares a number of hobbies with Gerald Knave, though he disagrees violently with Knave about politics, and about sex. (Knave's taste in women, he says, is regrettable. Nothing can be done about that, either.) Knave has had a great many odd adventures, and Mr. Janifer knows about some of them. Knave does a lot of talking (he says), so the knowledge is no great privilege; but it does seem to add to Mr. Janifer's small store of fun.

SURVIVOR

Laurence M. Janifer

ace books
A Division of Charter Communications Inc.
A GROSSET & DUNLAP COMPANY
1120 Avenue of the Americas
New York, New York 10036

SURVIVOR

An ACE Book

First Ace Printing: August 1977

Published simultaneously
in Canada

Printed in U.S.A.

DISCLAIMER #1:
The characters and situations in this book are entirely fictional. I'm damned if I know what the rest of us are, but I can make an unequivocal statement about the people and things in the book. I rejoice in the feeling of confidence that gives me.

DISCLAIMER #2:
The opinions of Gerald Knave, in this book, are not to be taken as expressing the opinions of the author. But if I were a betting man, that is the way I would set the odds.

The opinions of any of the other people or things in this book are not to be taken as expressing the opinions of the author, either. On that one, I'd call the odds no better than even, in the most promising cases.

This book is for
Remo and Chiun,
with my appreciation and respect;
and for Mr. Simon Templar,
our Onlie Progenitor,
with the deepest respect,
appreciation,
and affection.

PROLOGUE

Theirs was an older sun, an older planet. Five million years before the human race, the Vesci were already complex animals; already they lived in the swamplands they were to inhabit for millenia. They fed and drank and grew and reproduced and died. Like all life, they changed; but their change was not physical. As individuals, they were neither better nor worse than their competitors on the planet. A thousand times the race might have died as the seas shifted, as the winds came, as the great land animals of that world swept over their small colonies. A thousand times an accident occurred: they did not die. They lived and changed. One day, they woke.

They did not know how, they had little memory of the individual lives that had come to that awakening; the past was a dim cloud, and soon forgotten. They were born with their single awakening. They did not die: they proceeded to conquer their world.

Once (it is in the memory of the Vesci, which extends back in time to that awakening) a race of beings came to their world. They claimed it for themselves; they burned out the forests, piled the land with the animal dead, settled and built and were very greatly confident. For of that race it was true: what they did not destroy, they ruled. And they destroyed much, and were rulers over many. The world of the Vesci was a task for an idle afternoon; the task over, they made their dwellings and awaited the news of an enemy, somewhere, worthy of their time and their attention. While peace remained, they rested on the world of the Vesci, and complained that no challenge rose to stir their peculiar blood.

That race is dead. A remnant may exist, on some world human beings have never reached; somewhere a few may live and believe themselves conquerors. It is a big universe. But the race is dead; and it was on the planet of the Vesci that their death began.

They were great and wonderful fighters; but the Vesci do not fight. They were gifted in armament and the sciences of war and exploration; but the Vesci have never left their world, and have never built one single object.

They had no name (we gave them a name; they don't seem to mind); they had no science, no strategy, no weapons. They were the Vesci; and they were one being. The weapons and pretensions of another race meant nothing; like all the life on that planet, this new race could be made to join the Vesci, and become one being. They left their dwellings; they wandered aimless over the burned world; they neither ate nor reproduced—the Vesci, having in mind their history, did not think it necessary to tell them to do either. Soon they were gone.

A single being, staring at the stars. No human being can ever live from birth to death alone; there is no word to describe that state of solitude. The Vesci existed in that state: the quakes came, the volcanoes came, the continents of their world shifted and changed, some of the individuals died. Each was mourned (each is still mourned; we can not imagine how); the Vesci continued to live. A single being, staring at the stars.

The human race came out of a scattering of stars that had, for the Vesci, no particular pattern or name. The first ship flamed in the sky, and circled the world and landed. The second came, and the third. They were not alive: the Vesci turned away from them. The molar computers that were three First Site Exploration Ships of the great Comity of Planets reported through space-four to the keepers of master charts.

This world is habitable. This world is friendly. This world is (attached statistical tables: oxygen 1.01 Earth norm, temperature range .9 Earth normal, gravity 1.1 Earth normal—.9, .9, .9 Earth normal, a parade of wonders down the screens and the displayed pages)—this world is open to colonization.

This world holds no intelligent native race.

For the Vesci had turned away. They did not receive the reports; perhaps they would not have understood them. They waited, while the three ships gathered in their probes, their tests, their ambulating suspicious mechanisms. They waited while the three ships shut, and flamed, and went on into the sky. The ships had only slightly damaged the land; the land had repaired itself before, and would do so again. The land was of no great primary importance; Vesci did not live there.

Time passed. The first colonists came, the names for the histories. Goldberg and Issachwan, James and Lindorenyko, men and women and families, hesitantly, a few spilling out of a single ship at the first, then more and more. On the cleared land houses grew, and towns.

The planet had a mayor before it had a name, and then it was not a name of its own: they called it Cub IV, fourth planet of the star humanity called Hu-Li, the Fox.

Five years. Ten. Grain brought from the Comity seeds in and grows, the few Earth animals do well, there is a native mammal form very like a cow and the colonists learn to train it, use it for its milk and meat and labor. Open for colonization: it's a good world, Cub IV. Friendly and tame: the world without problems.

That was how they thought then, and how they lived. They heard of the ice troubles on Ponder, raggedly, at third hand from a cruising supply ship. They heard of the Native Treaty of Inoson, and the cost in blood and years. They heard of the battles of other worlds, and they walked in their own neat fields and smiled.

Ten years. Fifteen. They had named the seasons: it was in Spring that Johnny James came home one early afternoon, walked in the back door and sat down in a chair and never moved nor spoke of his own accord again. It was a bad thing, for a James to lose his mind like that; it showed, maybe, some weakness in the line. Though no one could be sure, and no one wanted to inquire. He was their single casualty in fifteen years: they put him in their small hospital and they tended him as well as they could. The robots made that easy, as they made the building easy: a home went up for each new family on Cub IV, and there were new homes all the time. Word of the planet without a problem got around. We were all a little proud of it; we thought we had reason to be.

Fifteen years. Twenty. Laia Kodorko stumbled through the dusty town street with her eyes wide open and her hands held out before her, hair and shift loose and looking like a blind woman, and she fifteen years old and healthy, strong as a grown woman too. The day was flat-hot with August sunlight (we had a ten-month year, we gave up February and December), no rains were due, the ground-effects cars swept dust from everywhere and left it flying over the streets of the city. Laia Kodorko stumbled forward, never blinking, her hands moving in flat arcs, her breath half-choked with the still air.

Tom Pedon ran out of a repairstore exit cradling a fax printer, and never looked up until he'd hit her and gone sprawling halfway down the short block. "Hey," he shouted, "you want to watch that—"

And the voice died in his throat. Laia went on walking. She did not turn, she did not stop. Tom stared after her. He was a man grown, nineteen Cub IV years; he stood up squaring his shoulders, cast round for his printer and found it in the dust, tucked it under one arm and ran again. Hailing her as he went; but she was silent.

"Hey, there, look now—" and he put his free hand on her shoulder. She stopped for that. Stopped: exactly. Still. She did not turn, nor move, nor make a sound.

Tom found that he was afraid to hold her, and afraid to let her go. He came round to the side, keeping his hand on her shoulder all the way. When he looked across into her face he saw her sleeping, both eyes wide in the dusty air and her face in entire repose. Johnny James had the same expression, but he had never seen Johnny James. Lots of people never went to the hospital at all.

He stared at her and the printer hit the ground and he never noticed that. He put up a hand to scrub at his dry lips. She was wearing a blue-striped red dress of a very old design. He said: "Hey, what's the matter? What happened? What can I do?"

Her head turned so slowly he had to blink to see it move. It was an absolutely steady motion, and he felt muscles pull with it in her shoulder. She moved nothing else until she was facing him directly. She had turned to him as exactly as a machine.

Her mouth opened and air hissed out. It closed again. Tom stood waiting. The sunlight had not changed. He began to feel cold. His lips dried and he wet them; they dried again. Her eyes were wider than any human eyes he had ever seen. There were eyes as wide as that in his dreams, he said later on; not often. She opened her mouth again.

"I am here. I have always been here. Get them all together to talk with me."

What frightened him the most (he said) was that she spoke his name. It did not seem as if she could be as she were, and speak his normal name.

"What's happened?" he said after a little silence.

"I am the second," she said. "There will be more. Perhaps all of you. We can not tell. And we can not be resisted."

At last her eyes shut; but when they opened there was nothing in them at all, nothing human. Tom took his hand off her shoulder as if it had gone red-hot, and hit her across the face. He knew that he was not hitting Laia Kodorko.

The mark was red on her cheek. She did not move. She said: "We can not be resisted."

Tom reached for her again, and then she moved. She went back, away from him down the dusty street. A single car went by on the other side and the wind whipped up. Two men came out of the back door of the Government Building, at the end of the street, talking together and using wide important gestures. Laia ran toward them, and Tom recovered his senses and came after her. Before she reached the men, as they turned to stare, he made a frantic wild swing from behind and clubbed her to the dust. The men—Nils Annal, Tobor Raisford—started toward her, astonished. Tom stood over her, shivering in the sunlight, as she shifted and rolled herself to face upward. Her empty eyes looked at the three men. She said: "We can not be resisted. Let me talk to them all."

Tom said: "It's alive. What ever made this——"

Nils Annal said: "Who does she want to talk to? What the Hell is this?"

"Everyone, Nils," she said. "Tobor. Tom. Get them all here. They should listen. I am the second."

Nils had seen Johnny James, and he remembered. Tobor said: "The second what?"

Nils looked at him, and looked at Tom. "We'll have to take her to the hospital," Nils said. "We have to know."

"I want to know right now," Tom said. He looked down at the eyes in the still face. "Who are you?" he said. "Who—made this?"

Laia's mouth opened. "We have no name," her voice said evenly. "We have never needed a name. Others need names. We are all. You may be the third, and then everyone. We can not tell."

Tom Pedon was nearly white; Tobor was staring, and

Nils Annal, who remembered Johnny James, began to shake. "The Hell you say," he told the thing on the ground. "Whatever kind of a monster——"

He stopped. His back arched, his arms went up in a wide circle. He was wearing a broadbrimmed black hat; his left hand knocked it off in that first motion. Then his eyes shut, and his arms went slowly out in front of him; he shook, and stilled, and opened his wide eyes. They watched his hands turn inward and approach his throat. The hands moved without check, touched the throat, and held. Both hands gripped tight. The eyes opened wider. Nils Annal opened his mouth in a great strain for breath. The hands did not relax until the eyes had closed, until the body was lying in the dust.

"We can not be resisted," the girl's voice said. "You may be the next. I must speak to them all."

It was after that they came to me.

I

My application had read *Gerald Knave: Survivor*. Some Earthstuck clerk with rimless glasses had asked me about it. "This space is supposed to list your profession."

"That's my profession, sonny," I'd said. He wasn't any younger than I was. That was how I felt about him. "I'm a survivor. I survive. I plan to do that on Cub IV."

"But—valued skills——"

"Sonny," I'd said, "you can take your valued skills and fold them until they are all corners. And then you can use your imagination until you find a way to dispose of them. No skill in this universe is worth thirty cents all by itself."

"Engineers," he said. "Farmers. Societal structuralists—government, banking systems——"

"Oh," I said. "I ought to make one exception. One skill that is worth the price, all by itself." I gave him a big wide smile. He pushed his glasses a little further up his nose. "Mine. Survival."

"But——"

"But nothing, sonny." I spoke to him gently. There are some people who will never believe they've been insulted unless they can remember a big rough voice. And he had to pass on the application, after all—so I'd decided to give him a lecture for free, but not bear down on him too much while doing the job. "The first thing your engineer has to know isn't engineering: it's survival. The first thing your societal structuralist has to know isn't—whatever societal structuralists call their field. It's survival. A dead specialist is not a useful specialist."

He blinked at me. "Well, of course, Sir," he said. "If you like to put it that way—but we try to select out for survivor types in all of our specialties. Now, if you——"

"You try," I said. "Sometimes you miss. I tell you what, sonny: you check my records. This isn't my first trip Out."

I sat in his office and waited. I had thirty hours before final clearance; there was no hurry. Better ways of spending my time; but no hurry. He went out and bustled around somewhere or other while I sat there, and after a while he came back. He looked impressed.

"Sir," he said. "I had no idea——"

"Well, now you have." The wait had made me a little edgy. "So if you'll put your okay on the forms——"

"The only thing I don't understand," he'd said, "is: why are you opting for Cub IV? That's the—the planet without a problem, they say. After Inoson, Secander—why Cub IV, Sir?"

I shrugged. "Call it a vacation," I said. "I use Earth as a base of operations: it's the only place in the universe with enough information for me to plan my next moves. But It's not much as a vacation spot: too crowded, and too old. I've got a space-four permissions card——" I had, and I might have been the only civilian who owned one; instantaneous rapid transit between systems is a limited privilege; but, as I'd shown several types like this clerk, though in higher governmental chairs, they never knew when they might need me. It seems I had this talent. What I called it on my application form.

"Of course, Sir. And—how long might your vacation be?"

"Five years," I said, more or less at random. In truth, it depended on when I got bored. Then, I told myself, I'd come drifting back to Earth, pick up some information, and head for whatever trouble seemed to be brewing. There was always action, if I wanted it.

Just then, I didn't want it. The simple life of a simple Cub IV citizen, maybe turning my hand to fax repair, or small-arms improvements (even a planet without a problem might have good hunting), maybe just vegetating on the allowance provided by a grateful, if that's the word, and it isn't, Comity.

"Certainly, Sir," he said.

"The forms," I said. He scribbled his name here and there, and put in a few decorations in those spaces that say Do Not Write Here. Must have given him a feeling of power. I said: "Thanks," which cost me nothing.

"You're very welcome, Sir," he said. Apparently, it occurred to me, my file on Earth was even more spectacular than I'd thought it would be. The little clerk was looking at me as if I'd discovered space-four, or come up with an endless supply of office cards nobody could fold, spindle or mutilate. Hero-worship is the term I'm groping for. "And—Sir, have a good vacation. Peace."

"Peace," I said; that year it was a semi-official

salutation around the offices. Again, it cost me nothing. And that was, after all, what I was looking for: peace, and a nice vacation.

So I'd come to Cub IV. And Johnny James had happened, and nobody'd bothered to tell me (and it wouldn't have meant anything, anyhow). And Laia Kodorko had happened, and there they were all over my living room, Tom Pedon and Tobor Raisford and the Governor that year, Malin Haddison. Malin was a middle-sized lumpy man with a talent for sweating, and a mind filled with large, predictable phrases. "You've got to do something," he told me in a voice that sounded like a middle reed stop on a good organ. "Some of us know you—know your record, anyhow. You have to help us out."

Well, I did, and I knew it. "Give me everything you have," I said. Tobor and Tom gave me the scene in the street. Malin gave me a lot of oratory, and some earnest sweat when his hand touched my arm.

"All right," I said. "This Laia Kodorko. I don't know her. Where is she now, and how can I get to her?"

Everybody talked at once. I held up my hands.

"One at a time. Tom?" I knew Pedon: an excitable sort, a man who did everything at a dead run whether that was the best way to manage it or not, but a friendly sort too, and an honest reporter. Most people tell you what they think you'd like to hear. Half the time, they hypnotize themselves into believing it as well. It's not a helpful trait.

Tobor and Malin shut up. Everybody looked at Tom.

"She's standing right there," he said. His voice

4

shook a little bit. It must have been a scene, there in the middle of an afternoon street. "She said she was waiting. She said we would all have to come and hear her."

"Did she say how long she was going to wait?"

Tom rubbed his hands against his cheeks. "She didn't say—much of anything else. She kept telling us she couldn't be resisted. Or they couldn't be resisted. She kept talking—not like Laia. Not like anybody human."

"So she's still there," I said. "And Nils is dead. You're sure of that?"

They all nodded. "He—choked himself," Tom said. "I didn't think anybody could do that—all by himself. Choked himself to death."

"Nobody can do it," I said, "not with his bare hands. Not all by himself." I looked at them, and I got up out of my nice, comfortable chair, and I pushed the buzzer hung at my waist. "Apparently," I said, "he had help."

There was a little silence. Tobor said: "They."

"They," I agreed. "Them. Whoever, or whatever, Laia Kodorko is talking about." My Totum arrived in the doorway. I turned to him for a second. "I'm going out. I don't know when I'll be back. Keep a state of readiness, and keep out all the normal alarms. File anything that happens until I return, but don't give me the results until I ask for them." He waited, looking, as always, like a five-foot-tall human being, basketball-player build, made out of stainless steel. "Effective immediately," I said. "Other than that, you're on your own."

"Yes," he said. They build some of them now to say

5

"Yes, Master." I never took to it. A good GP Factotum is an extra hand, he's not a slave.

I turned back to the others. "Lead the way," I said. At the door I reached over and grabbed a sticktite holster with a handsize cannon in it. Tobor looked at me.

"You never can tell," I said. "I might meet something worth shooting."

He didn't think that was very funny. Well, damn it, neither did I. A perfectly good vacation spoiled —because the planet without a problem had turned out to have one after all. And a sizable one, at that, to judge from immediate indications.

The door shut behind us. The street where Laia Kodorko was waiting was no more than ten minutes' walk from that door.

We started off. Tobor and Tom led the way for about ten steps; then we were all bunched up; after that I was in front, all by my little lonesome.

Malin was very helpful. He told me which way to turn, and how many blocks.

When we were within fifteen feet of Laia—she was standing there, totally at ease, totally relaxed, Nils at her feet, and she was looking straight at us—when we got within fifteen feet, to the corner of the street, Malin jumped me from behind.

II

I went with him, falling forward and flipping him over my head. He hadn't expected that; most people

6

don't react that fast. But he was fast, too: he lit rolling and came back at me before I could draw the damned handgun.

His hands were stretched out as if he were going to try for my neck, so I took the opportunity, grabbed one wrist and stepped to the side, and swung him straight into Laia Kodorko's path.

Of course she'd been heading for me too.

He hit and, off balance, they both went sprawling. I went for the gun again, faster, and got it out before Laia was on her feet. Malin was already up, standing poised for a second try.

I didn't shoot him dead.

That's what makes me a survivor, I think. I don't like to kill. And what a survivor generally needs isn't death; it's information

Tobor Raisford and Tom Pedon were ranged behind me. Everything up to that time had taken maybe thirty seconds, and they'd got that far. I thought maybe the two of them could take care of Laia if Malin came at me again, and I had few worries, facing one man with a gun ready in my hand. I don't like to kill; but I'm not, you could say, prejudiced on the subject.

Malin took a very slow step forward. I didn't shoot, and I didn't lower the gun. The street was in the shade of very early evening, and the shadows made him look like some kind of clay figure, barely human. I couldn't see the expression on his face, but I didn't have to; it would have been a great surprise to find out that he'd had one.

The others hadn't. Not from what I'd heard.

And Malin was one of the others. Not on the way in, or he'd have tried to take me before—maybe in my own house, with enough weapons around so there'd have been one or two for him. And not before he got to my house, or he'd have brought a weapon. Most of the way, he'd been Malin Haddison, good old lumpy Malin, Governor that year because he wanted the job and had, they tell me, a certain talent for administration.

Now, obviously, he was—something else.

He took another step. Behind me, Tobor and Tom shifted nervously. I said, as quietly as I could: "If he tries for me, go for the girl." Laia was still lying on the ground.

Maybe Malin didn't hear me. I wasn't sure. He took another step. The gun was a little slippery in my hand. I didn't move it, and I didn't use it.

Four steps away from me he flung himself sideways, landed on all fours like a cat, and sprang back at me—from that position, and from one side.

It wasn't a human motion. It was possible; it just didn't happen. Anyhow, I'd never seen it before.

I didn't waste any time admiring it. He came for me clawing, and I sidestepped and used the gun at last: I banged him on the side of the head with it as he went by. He kept going, but when he landed he landed flat, and he stayed that way.

All this time, there was a lot of noise going on. I looked around to see Tobor and Tom hanging on to Laia Kodorko, one man to each arm. She'd got up, all right, and she was heading for me, too. They call it hysterical strength; she was tossing two big men around, keeping them entirely off balance, just about banging them into

8

each other for a finish, and coming at me, at fair speed, all at the same time.

She might have been able to handle two men. She couldn't handle three. I banged her on the head when I got close to her—same as I had Malin, but I had a little more time, and judged it a little better. Malin could wake up with a concussion, I thought; Laia would just wake up.

And what were they going to be, either of them, when they did wake up? I took off my belt and looped it around Malin's ankles. Tom got the idea and tied Laia's ankles with his belt. Tobor took his shirt off, tore it in two, and we used the halves to tie both pairs of wrists behind their owners' backs.

Then we just stood there and waited.

I don't know why: nobody came along. We don't really have a busy town, but we don't have a deserted one, either. Apparently nobody was looking out a window, and nobody was using that street.

Maybe that was a good thing. I rather think it was; we didn't need any more of what Malin, and Laia—and Johnny James?—had turned into, and the odds were about even that we'd have got them. All told, there had been six human beings in that street. Now there was Tobor, and Tom, and me; and Laia, and Malin, and —in the dust, so still he'd been entirely forgotten during the action—Nils Annal, or what was left of him. Three of us, and three of—them.

As I say, the odds were just about even.

We waited. Evening came down. We don't have street lighting yet; we'll build it when we need it, but a

9

farming community is an early-to-bed community, and it just hadn't come up as high priority. I began to wish for it. If we were still there when it got really dark, and if someone else, walking into the street, happened to get—taken over . . .

Tobor Raisford surprised me. He took a big grenade-shaped container from his belt, set it in the dust, and pulled a ring on the top. The thing lit up.

"Handlamp," he said. "I carry it everywhere. You never know."

My God, you never did, I told him. What Tobor never knew was how close he came to getting a hole punched through him. It's a Hell of a design for a lamp: anything that looks like a big grenade damn well ought to act like a big grenade.

I suppose some idiot on Earth thought it was a cute idea. I wonder if it ever *has* got anybody killed, in tight circumstances, without the chance to explain? Would they hush it up, or would they change the design?

Damned if I know.

The light cast wild, dancing shadows all around us, in the street and up onto the dark fronts of the buildings. Laia and Malin and Nils were three still mounds, two of them breathing.

In a little while Laia came to. She tried to sit up, found out she was tied hand and foot, and rolled over onto her back. In the light of Tobor's lamp, her face wasn't remotely human: it was absolutely motionless, absolutely passionless. Something stared out of it at me. It wasn't anything I'd ever imagined before.

Nobody said anything for a minute or two. Laia didn't move; she only waited. She kept watching me—whatever she was, and whatever she had to watch with.

I said: "Who are you?"

Her voice wasn't Laia's, either. I'd never heard Laia's voice, but it must have been human. This one was flat and quiet. My Totum sounds more lifelike than she did.

"We are here."

"All right," I said. "Fine. You're here. Who are you?"

"We have always been here." I got the feeling she was trying to answer my question in a language that wasn't built for it. The thing she had—turned into, maybe—didn't have any words for *who*, or for any particular identity at all. Who are you? The things that have always been here; maybe that was as close as she could get.

"What do you want?" That had to be answerable. If it lives, it wants something; that one is either a universal rule or a definition, if there's any way of telling the difference.

"We want everyone to hear."

An audience. Nothing new, and the answer I deserved; that's what she'd told Tobor and Tom.

"When you get everybody together," I said, "what do you want to tell them?"

Her eyes blinked. It was not a human gesture. Eyes have to blink; it's a lubricating device. That was the way she made it look. "That we are here, and we have been here before any human being came to this place," she said. Back to square one, I thought.

"Anything else?"

"We can not be resisted," she said. She was lying tied on the ground, and so was Malin, but I knew what the voice meant. Laia hadn't been able to resist what had happened to her, and neither had Malin.

Neither had Nils.

Apparently the rest of us had. It was an interesting datum, when you looked at it: whatever we'd resisted, we hadn't even noticed.

They hadn't tried to take us all?

Why not?

I didn't have enough facts to make conclusions out of. I tried to collect some more.

"Why do you want everyone to hear this?"

Her eyes blinked again. Malin was awake, I noticed, but he didn't move; he didn't even test his bonds. Whatever he was, he'd known he was tied before he woke up.

"We want them to hear," that voice said, "so they will leave the planet."

I can't say it came as a surprise. I don't suppose my answer did, either.

"But we like the planet," I told her. "And we damn well intend to stay on it. You can talk as long as you like; it won't change that."

They knew human beings, that much was clear; they'd taken over language, muscles and a whole array of facts from at least three minds. They knew the answer they'd get to a nice, simple request to leave the party.

One day, maybe, a human outpost will agree to get off a world it's colonized.

The human race will start dying on that day.

We might be nicer beings if that weren't so; but

there's one thing we wouldn't be. We wouldn't be human.

Laia shouldn't have been surprised. I don't know what I expected for an answer. What I got was total collapse.

She sagged in her bonds; her eyes closed and she went limp. She looked like a puppet with its strings cut.

Tobor and Tom each took a step toward her, and I waved them back. I didn't move.

Laia opened her eyes—wide and full. Her back arched and she went as rigid as she could, heels and shoulders and head touching the ground and nothing else. Her heels drummed on the ground. She began to scream—a high, wavering sound like a siren. It chopped off as she took in a long breath, and began again.

I waved the others back again. I walked toward her, slowly. I kept Malin in the corner of my eye, but he was out of the picture; I'd tied those knots myself. After the first two steps I ignored him.

Laia was spasming, beating at the ground with her heels, with her fists, her eyes wide open and her mouth pulled wide by that long, inhuman scream . . .

I reached her. I knelt down to touch her. She gave no sign that she knew I was there. I cut her legs loose. The spasming continued; she hit me with her side, drew another breath, started another scream. I cut her hands loose.

She made a grab for my gun. There'd been no pause. As soon as her hands were free the spasms stopped and the noise stopped and her hands went for my gun.

It wasn't there. I was up on my feet; as she turned, getting to her knees, I hit her backhanded.

She went back a little ways, and down. I got the gun

in my own hand again, but she stood up very slowly, and she didn't try to come for me.

"Come on," I said. "Come at me. Let's see why you can't be resisted."

Whatever they were, you couldn't make them angry, either. You had to figure them out on the run.

She looked at all three of us, very calmly, with that still face that wasn't human any more.

"There will be others," she said. "Johnny James will help."

I hadn't really needed that confirmation.

"He is helping already," she said.

I showed her the gun and told her to kneel down in a hurry. I got Tobor and Tom to retie her while I held the gun. She didn't fight.

When I had them both secure, and propped up against the back of the Government Building, I turned my back on them: they'd keep.

What Johnny James was probably doing wouldn't.

III

I tried to make a little sense on the way out to the hospital—it was on the edge of town, a nice long lope, and I began to wish for the first time that any one of us had thought of a ground-effects car. Mine was sitting quietly in its little garage, but I'd have been perfectly willing to take Tobor's, or Tom's, or lift one that happened to be parked nearby. It's a trustful community; I may be the only person in it who makes a habit of locking all doors and means of access. How first-generation colonies ever manage to survive is sometimes beyond me—but then, Cub IV had been the planet without a problem, hadn't it?

Past perfect tense, and it very nearly had been. There is no such tense as the present perfect—there being no such thing.

All right: Johnny James and Laia Kodorko had been taken over by—something. Apparently not physical, since Nils Annal (by report) and Malin Haddison had been grabbed in the same way, nothing physical being noted, and damned little being possible.

Mental takeover. Telepathy.

Telepathic aliens, wiping out the minds of human beings and replacing them with their own minds—no, strike that. Their own mind: Laia said *we*, but everything sounded like a packet of all-identical beings, and a difference that makes no difference is no difference: if they're all alike, they're all one thing.

Maybe a telepathic race would have to be all one thing. Nobody knows how telepathy works, or even what it is—for all we do know, ants are telepathic, and that's why they act the way they do—but it sounds reasonable.

A telepathic race that had lived on Cub IV since long before the first human colony got planted. . . .

And remained hidden from the survey ships?

That, I told myself, was an interesting point.

And only took over about half the available minds in a given area—maybe only those four minds on the whole planet? (After all, the colony had been there twenty years!)

That was an even more interesting point. If the only

15

locus of trouble at the hospital were going to be Johnny James, we had no real need to hurry; my God, the mechs were programmed to take care of anything an individual patient might see fit to do, and any fit he might feel like throwing. Let alone what the human doctors and attendants could contribute . . .

I think I half expected to find the hospital a peaceful place. Maybe I was still hoping, somewhere, that my vacation plans would stand up.

Well: it's a nice white cube, four stories high, quite a lot of it nice one-way-reflective glass brick, which goes a long way toward solving the heating problem and makes the building look rather like an enormous single die with an incredible number of spots on it—the one-way-reflectives are a nice solid black from outside.

They are also very nearly unbreakable. And the building is, more or less by accident, a fair job of soundproofing.

So we didn't hear much until I pushed open the swinging double doors at the entrance.

Tobor and Tom crowded in behind me. The shrieks and the crashes came down the cavernous lobby like a welcoming committee. Johnny James was not alone up there.

Suppose (I asked myself) these telepaths, whatever they are, can take over mechanicals?

It didn't sound probable, and it was easily the most horrible idea I could come up with. I stuffed it back into its little pocket on the Ignore side of my skull, and took a fast scan around the lobby.

Stairs heading up on my right, stairs heading up (and marked *Down*) on my left. A sort of artificial lake-

and-garden dead ahead of me, meant to give the hospital a cheerful appearance or something.

Not a human being in sight.

I started up the right-hand stairs—why fight City Hall when there are so many other fights going on?—and heard Tobor and Tom come up behind me; I didn't look around to see.

Which was lucky, or I'd have been hit by the damn bed.

Somebody—two somebodies, at least—had picked up a massive hospital bed, loaded with mech attachments and extras and optionals, and weighing about the same as a standard model car. What it had been used for until I came along I didn't know then—reconstructing from later evidence, I'd say a combination battering-ram and superman-sized quarterstaff—but as I came up the stairs it changed function and became a missile.

I flung myself to one side. Behind me Tobor found time to rip out one curse. The bed went straight down the stairway, hitting about four steps from the bottom and taking a large hunk of stair with it as it bounced off and shuddered itself into the artificial lake.

Somebody up there didn't like me.

I looked up, clinging as far to the side of the stair as I could; it had solid banisters four feet high, which felt like an advantage.

Two men and a woman were standing at the top of the stairs, looking down.

None of them were human. None of them were Johnny James, either.

One of the men, and the woman, were doctors.

So much for peace and quiet.

17

They didn't look as if lugging the bed around had tired them any. I went on up another few steps, my following still coming along behind, and the mad trio started down.

I had collected a fact that didn't fit, but I had no idea what it was. I didn't have any time to worry it out, either. The male doctor jumped for me, and I sidestepped and he banged into the banister and began to roll slowly down the stairs. Tom Pedon got hastily out of his way and let him go down.

That reduced the immediate odds.

We went up in a hurry, though the two up there were set for us, and barely managed to make it to the top. I grabbed the other male as he came for me, and Tom grabbed the female doctor. They were on intersecting courses; we helped them along.

The crash put them out of action. But by then we had four more people coming at us.

One of them was carrying a floor-lamp. It made a Hell of a good quarterstaff all by itself. One small glancing blow with it and I was going to be out of the picture.

So I drew the man's attention, faded back as he began to swing the lamp—grabbed it as it came at me (possible, once I was going back in the same direction it was travelling, reducing its relative speed), and yanked it high.

The man at the other end went up and over; he hadn't had all *that* good a grip on the thing.

Tobor was yelling something inaudible in the general din. I stole one look around and saw him struggling with a patient—Tobor was slowly winning out, but the patient, a broken-arm case, kept trying to club him over the head with his cast.

Tom Pedon was somewhere else. I couldn't locate him in one scan, and didn't have time for two.

I began to notice that the fight had begun long before we'd hit the hospital.

In other words, we were in the same sort of spot we'd been in out on the street: some takeovers, some passovers. And the passovers, probably taken a little aback to begin with, were fighting back.

On our side.

I began to gain ground. The emergency stair to the next two floors was fifty yards down a hallway. I made the fifty yards, leaving a trail of bodies and hospital equipment—no dead that I could notice, but few conscious.

I reached the door marked Stair and yanked it open. The stairwell smelled as musty as they always do, everywhere and anywhere, with the slight addition of some sharp chemical: hospital purifier.

Behind me, patients and doctors (and Tobor and Tom) were battling insanely with each other. Chaos reigned; the place looked as if somebody had taken two pre-Space TV series (the flat ones), a doctor series and a Godzilla-destroys-the-World series, and shuffled them.

Hell of a way to run a hospital. I shut the door behind me and started up the stairs.

I didn't hear any footsteps but my own. Apparently either I'd been the first to think of this particular notion,

19

or somebody was too far ahead of me to matter . . . or there was something wrong with the notion. After all, was I absolutely *sure*. . . .

No. But outside the stairwell, people were bashing each other over nothing at all—a real, authentic chaos: nobody seemed to have any motive beyond making massive trouble.

I hit the third-floor landing and went on up. One floor to go.

Halfway up the last flight, I saw the fourth-floor door yank open. A man stood in the doorway holding a handful of—somethings. He grabbed one and threw it at me like a spear.

IV

It was a hypo—loaded. I heard it splash and trickle on the wall behind me.

My gun was already out. Small miracle: nobody had grabbed it out of my holster down there in the first rounds. He tossed a second hypo. I moved an inch; his aim was improving.

He got no third chance. I hit him in the shoulder. He went down—my handgun packs as much power as the makers consider possible. Why make do? The basic model is the preSpace .45 Magnum automatic, and it throws the same solid slug.

The fourth floor was mostly Operating Theatre, and mostly deserted. My spear-tosser lay in the doorway and I stepped over him, gun still out, but I saw nothing else dangerous. Two people, both in whites, lay unconscious on the floor, which made the question of whose side they were on academic. I didn't hear any noises.

I went into the Theatre. Deserted, which was a relief; I'd been picturing a nice bloody fight over the body of a slightly carved patient. And Operating Theatre mechs are walking disasters if you want to program them wrong.

I went to the far wall, located the small glass box, punched it in with the butt of my gun, and pulled the handle.

Then I headed—fast—for the resuscitation equipment, strapped an oxygen mask over my mouth and nose, and cracked the bottle. Pure oxy wouldn't really do me any particular good, but for a brief while I could stand it—and I could just manage to carry the bottle with me back down the stairs.

I waited four minutes. The most conservative theory says three will do.

I got up, with the bottle in port-arms position, and went on down the stairs. Everything was very quiet.

It was a three-hour gas with a half-hour lifespan. Meaning: once it got you, you were out for three hours; but if it were diffused through the hospital (which was what that handle inside the glass box had been all about) it would stay around for half an hour before (I'd been given to understand) converting itself into CO_2, nitrogen, helium and a variety of teeny byproducts, all nontoxic.

So for half an hour (correction: forty minutes; I am

always, always conservative about other people's conservative estimates) I went round the place carrying that damn bottle and its successor—it is never very hard to find a new oxygen bottle in a hospital. In that time I tried to begin doing the only job that made sense: separating out, among the fallen figures, our side from their side. The good guys from the bad guys.

The humans from the—whatever. The takeovers. The things whose only name seemed to be We-who-have-been-here-always.

After that, I got rid of the bottle (still better than half full; I shut it carefully and stacked it away) and the mask and did the job a little faster.

Tobor and Tom were the two I was sure of. Everybody else was a guess, even the people who'd been fighting me on the way up—even the man I'd shot.

Who had he thought *I* was?

I did have a small basis for selection. Human beings tended to act like human beings—and it was a sure bet that they hadn't started the fight.

Anyone unconscious in his or her bed was probably human, caught by surprise.

On the other hand, anyone using weapons with real damaging power—our friends with the semiportable bed, and the man with the lamp, among a good many examples I turned up—was likely to be one of the bad guys. Humans who work in a hospital do not tend to use more force than necessary in a fight—they've seen too much damage, and they don't want to see any more.

Offhand, a doctor in a fight is likelier to kill you than to give you severe, messy damage.

The human beings I left alone, for the most part.

22

The others—the ones I thought were others—I trussed up. Using anything available—bed sheets, hospital gowns, rubberoid tubing—you name it. I used the wiring from that lamp, for instance.

And at the end of three hours of damned hard work I had three groups of people. The almost-certainly-humans—the almost-certainly-something-elses—and about half the people in the hospital, staff and patient (and an occasional visitor), the no-decisions. The cases where I didn't even have enough facts for a *stupid* guess.

I had done the Hell of a lot of lugging.

Mostly, I'd done it with the no-decisions. I'd put them all on one floor, the lobby, and tried to block both staircases with assorted debris. That group was fairly certain to break into more chaos when it woke up; I did my best to limit it.

I got Tobor and Tom, who'd both been very busy on the second floor when the sleepy signal hit their nerve centers, comfortable near the Charge Station, sitting up against the outer railing. (That reminds me of the one other person I was certain of: Johnny James. I'd found him easily enough, in a tangle on the third floor, let out of his very private little room by some Something-confederate with the keys. I tied him and left him; he seemed to me no more, and no less, important than any of the others.)

After all, if they were all alike. . . .

Of course, not everybody woke up at the same time. People are physically variable; and as long as the aliens were inside people, they were physically variable, too. I made sure to be on the second floor with Tobor and

Tom—and a few other people I'd selected as probable-human, and dragged over for company —when the deadline hit, and as everybody began to come to I heard some sounds of battle begin down in the lobby below.

Begin—and end.

Tom looked at me as if he had suddenly come up with the great-grandfather of all hangovers. Most sleep-gas does leave you a little that way, and I felt suitably sorry for him. "What happened?" he asked me.

I did notice that one thing: he assumed I knew. My reputation was getting around . . . but I'd known that when he'd first shown up, along with the others: why come to me, except for the fact that I was who I was? *Gerald Knave: Survivor.*

Times, now and then, I wished I'd lied on that application.

Why hadn't I put down Accountant, for instance? Or Fish Breeder?

Ah, well. "Sleep gas," I said. "It was the only way to stop the damn fight."

He blinked. "You set off the pumps?"

"Sure."

"How'd you know?"

I shrugged. "Came to the hospital when I first got here, like everybody else," I said; "orientation and on-the-spot physicals. And I got curious. I asked a lot of questions. I got some answers."

"Why?"

"Curiosity is a survival trait," I said. "What a survivor needs is facts. All sorts of facts." Then I realized he hadn't been asking that question. "Why does a hospital have a sleepy-gas setup? Suppose a pandemic nobody suspected was there was suddenly isolated? Suppose there were an accident and it got loose? Hospital's where it would happen. If you had to immobilize everybody, fast—no matter what condition they were in, no matter whether they felt like listening to you or not—how would you do it?"

"And what happens when everybody wakes up?"

I shrugged again. "You've got things a little straightened out. Maybe you can shoot yourself full of antidote—I didn't get those answers, any more than I got the location of every sleepy-gas handle in the place; there must be several, but somebody mentioned the one in the Operating Theatre. Me, I rigged an oxygen mask."

"For three hours?"

"Forty minutes," I said. "The gas dissipates after—" The Hell with it. Everybody was awake and everybody was asking questions. If I started answering them I'd spend the next three days giving lectures. Downstairs, the fighting that had started was dying down. Like Laia Kodorko, the Somethings down below had decided to be sensible.

Whatever it was they meant by sensible.

It was one more interesting fact.

And filing it reminded me of another—of the one that had bothered me, coming up the stairs.

I'd found more probable-humans among the doctors and attendants, more probable-Somethings among the patients. And that (somehow) made sense to me; it was one end of a buried train of logic.

Two doctors and a patient coming at us from the

second-floor landing with that bed had reversed the relationship, I'd thought. And that had bothered me; that was wrong.

There should have been more humans, more people the aliens didn't, or hadn't, or couldn't take over, among the hospital staff than among the patients.

I knew that perfectly well. It had that satisfying feel of a piece fitting in to a large puzzle.

But I didn't know why. And when I'd looked at it for a minute, I discovered I didn't have even the faintest beginning of a notion.

Well, it would wait. It would damned well have to.

There was a depressing amount of work to be done—most of it lectures, at that.

V

I ended up down in the lobby.

Tobor and Tom and I had rounded up most of the probable-humans, and headed them down, either by the stairs or by the elevators. (Sure the hospital had elevators. But when people are using hospital equipment to fight with, you use stairs; an elevator is a damn small box on the end of a damn long string. Happily, nobody had wrecked them during the chaos— oversight, I supposed—so some people saved a little vertical walktime.) I had a lot of second thoughts about cutting loose the probable-Somethings, and finally decided against it: let them stay where they were.

If they were all linked to the same mind—or all shared the same link, however it went—then the Some-things in the lobby would be passing on the news as it happened, and it didn't matter where the other Some-things were. If there wasn't a single mind-link—well, then nothing that had happened made even the limited amount of sense I was willing to grant it.

The only worry was the probable-Somethings I'd misjudged, who were really human beings. And there was nothing to be done about them, just then.

There is, after all, damn it, a limit to neatness.

When everyone was collected in the lobby, with exceptions as just noted, I climbed up four or five steps on the Down staircase, the one the flying bed hadn't damaged, and yelled for silence.

Nobody was really making very much noise. I got my silence.

For a second, then, I looked them over.

Some I'd seen before. Some bore the distinguishing marks of famous families—those I could recognize the way I'd recognized Johnny James; the Lindorenyko size and shape, the James nose and so on. Some were total strangers.

But those divisions didn't mean anything, not any more.

Some were human. The faces looking at me had human expressions of a nice, wide variety: curiosity, interest, anger, discouragement, annoyance, and a lot more.

Some were smooth masks. Whatever looked out from behind the eyes of nearly half that group seemed passionless, unmoving, and absolutely uninterested in anything except its own wishes.

Do all telepaths have to be self-centered? Is it a necessary condition that a telepath suffer from the sin of Pride? Sounds as if it makes sense.

Whatever it was, it made a nice cool wind blow down my back when I looked at it, staring up at me through nearly a hundred faces.

"You've stopped fighting," I said. "That shows some sense."

"We have suspended activity for the present," a voice said. Male or female, what difference did it make?

"All right," I said. "Then let me explain to the human beings." That drew a mutter—mostly from the human beings. Some of them apparently hadn't had time to put the pieces together.

Of course, I had a few more pieces to begin with: Laia Kodorko had given me those.

"The people you're fighting aren't people any longer," I said. "I don't know if they can ever be people again." I waited for another voice from the crowd. Nobody felt like enlightening me. Very well; for *alien* read *intelligent alien*. The first rule of intelligence: never give information away for free, if you think you might make somebody pay for it.

Most people aren't intelligent, thank God.

"Cub IV is inhabited. It's been inhabited since long before we ever got here—even the first of us. There is an indigenous, intelligent race." That drew more mutters. "What they look like, or even where they are, I have no idea. But their powers seem to be mental. What they can do is take over the human mind."

And that is a scare-statement of a very high order.

28

People began to move around, talking to each other. Somebody shouted up, in a human voice:

"Mine? My mind?"

A nice male tenor, and undoubtedly a doctor, probably a surgeon; surgeons tend to have good enunciation—maybe they need it to get through to Operating Theatre personnel—and those three words had to be beautifully enunciated to be distinguished at all over a general murmur. I like appreciating small successes like that, when I can; it gives me a feeling of luxury. As if I had the time to notice such things.

Which, I reminded myself, I did not have. "Not yours, friend," I said. "You're human—your voice proves it. Look around; is there anybody who can't tell the difference?"

More talk and shuffling. The point got across.

Somebody said, loudly enough for me to hear: "Johnny James."

"Right," I said. "And Laia Kodorko, and Nils Annal, and Malin Haddison. And a lot of others right here. Apparently the aliens can only take over certain minds; others seem to be closed tight."

"Why?"

"I have no idea," I said, which was inaccurate. I had an idea. Hell, I *knew* why. But the knowledge was buried somewhere. It had something to do with everything I'd seen—with the fact, for instance, that more doctors than patients had turned up as good guys. But it was no time to turn the place into a discussion group. "For some reason, they waited twenty years to make their move—except for Johnny James. Call him a test, a prologue, something like that. And now they've made it. Here in this hospital, nearly half of you—patients, staff and visitors—is an alien telepathic being, or an alien telepathic network, if there's any difference.''

A voice. Not human. ''Not only in the hospital.''

''Everywhere,'' I said. ''All right. I got the message; maybe you haven't heard it yet. The message is: get out. Leave the planet. We are kicking you off.''

The next voice had to be human. The aliens, remember, were intelligent. ''But they can't *do* that!'' somebody said, with instant indignation.

''They damn near wrecked this hospital,'' I said. ''I don't know why—maybe just to prove a point——''

''We can not be resisted,'' an alien voice said.

I nodded. ''That's what they keep telling me,'' I said. ''That's what they want you to believe. They can't be resisted, so if they say Go, friend, you go.''

Mutters. Some moving around. Tobor's voice: ''So what do we do? Pack up and leave?''

I looked them over. Nobody's face looked decisive. ''I don't think there will be any interference with anybody who wants off,'' I said. ''I think standard clearances will be arranged just as rapidly as possible. Those of you who came from Earth, or from one of the high-civilization Comity worlds, will almost certainly not be going back there—you got out of the crowd, friend, and that's the way they want it—but you can probably take your pick of the newer spots. Inoson, for instance. A lot of them.''

''Why should any of us stay?'' one voice said belligerently.

I suppose it was a human voice. ''We're here. We're not going to leave because some alien being waves a danger flag at us. You may be different—all right, get out. Get your clearances and pick another planet. But I warn you——''

''Warn me? Of what?'' The belligerence was still there. One of the odd things about human beings is that pacifists are the most dedicated fighters in the race. They just don't fight with physical weapons, and have managed to make themselves (and some others) believe that, therefore, they don't fight at all. But if you've ever been in an argument with a real, convinced, dedicated pacifist. . . .

I'd recognized the tone. ''Wherever you go, you're going to have to fight. You won't live for free; you knew that when you shipped out.''

''But——''

''I know: you shipped out to Cub IV. The planet without a problem. Which, friend, is a contradiction in terms. We're just beginning to find that out—we should all have known it twenty years ago, and got suspicious enough to look for the catch in this paradise; we might have found it sooner and licked it faster. But it had to be here; it has to be anywhere.'' I sighed. This was the sort of lecturing that made me tired; the careful laying-out of the obvious. ''The Romans said: If you want peace, prepare for war. You've heard of the Romans?'' A general mutter. ''Fine. The truth is, if you want anything whatever, prepare for war—of one kind or another, against one sort of enemy or another. If you want something—from oxygen to breathe to the latest 3V tape epic to forget with—there's something in the universe that doesn't want you to have it, and will fight like Hell to keep you from getting hold of it.''

"But—intelligent beings. . . ."

"We lived here twenty years," I said. "We didn't bother them—or they'd have popped up before now. Whatever part of the world they use is a part we haven't even bothered to survey closely enough to find them. We could live here, as far as I can see now, for twenty thousand years and not disturb them any more than we did in all this time."

"Maybe they just had to wait until——"

"Maybe anything," I said. I was getting a little impatient. "But they didn't just open negotiations with us. They didn't start in peace. They took over one mind years ago—and then waited, and took over another today. Laia Kodorko. When they were interrupted, they took over a third mind—Nils Annal's—and used it to kill Nils with. I call that a declaration of war; whatever these beings are, they're not looking for a peaceful solution. They're not looking for a compromise, or even for any real talk. They're perfectly willing to begin by wiping out as many of us as they can reach —which is what they tried to do here, just as a demonstration. Which is what they may be doing elsewhere——"

"Not at the moment," an inhuman voice cut in. I nodded to it, somewhere out there in the crowd.

"For this relief much thanks." I looked around for the pacifist. I couldn't find him. I didn't try very hard. "At any rate: we've had our demonstration. Anybody who hasn't been taken over is apparently immune—that's not something to bank on, but it'll do until we get some more facts."

"And if we don't want to leave?" somebody shouted. A woman after my own heart, bless her.

"Why, then, we follow me," I said. "The others of you: go home, and barricade yourselves in. Fast. And watch your backs on the way—how long the truce is on, I can't say. Flip the Community radio on, and leave it on; the batteries are good for a couple of years. And wait."

"For what, Knave?" somebody shouted. Tom Pedon.

"For me," I said. "I'll be in touch. We're going to have to figure out what to do."

"And who elected you Big Chief?" that brass-voiced lady asked.

I spread my hands. "I did," I said. "And the people who know me, and know my reputation. Malin Haddison's your Mayor—but Malin isn't Malin any more; turns out he wasn't immune."

Lots of muttering and stirring.

Well, it was almost over.

"Tom," I called, "I want you up here. The rest: get home if you can. Barricade and wait. I'll be in touch as soon as I can—and it won't be long; we can't afford that."

A new voice asked: "What about the patients?"

The inhuman faces staring up at me gave me no clue. "I have no idea," I said. "Some—most, probably—can't be moved. They'll need care. But the hospital can't really be barricaded, not successfully; this lobby is too easy to breach." I looked around at them. "Anybody who wants to stay and care for the patients deserves a medal, and the rest of us will see he—or she—gets one. If we live."

Somebody said: "But—" and shut up as his brain caught up with his mouth.

33

There wasn't anything else to ask; there wasn't anything else I could tell them.

Slowly, the crowd started to disperse. It interested me very much that the takeovers, the inhumans, were leaving the hospital just like the human beings: there would be fights on the way back to town or the way out to the farm.

Mass attack hadn't worked; now they were thinking about one-on-one.

That wasn't going to work much better, I told myself; one-on-one is an automatic disadvantage for a telepath, who can't be used to it. But some more humans were going to be hurt, going to die. . . .

Lots more, I thought, if I stood there brooding about it. Tom was standing next to me.

"I want to go over some names with you," I said. "It seems to me we'll need about six people. Maybe less—and the less the better."

"Six people?" he said. "For what?"

He was fast on his feet; his mind was a little slower. Well, I hadn't wanted him for his mind. "Call it a command post, or a guerrilla crew," I said. "A raiding party, maybe. But—somebody's going to have to carry the fight for the colonists, Tom; and whatever we can persuade the rest of the citizens to do, I have the feeling you and I are elected to get out in front."

He looked at me with a sort of mirthless glee: a big, rawboned redhead with deep-sunk eyes. A sort of young, auburn Lincoln, without the beard or the axe. "I thought you were a survivor, Knave."

"I am," I said. "And it's Jerry." I sighed. "It's just that, now and again, I have to prove it."

VI

We did not walk back to my place.

That was a decision that took very little thought. Tom had borrowed a car from one of the visitors we'd tabbed as probable-human—I had to keep that "probable" in there because all the Somethings I had seen acted like total aliens, or ill-trained zombies, but I couldn't be sure that every single one was going to act like that; maybe a few might be well enough trained, or well enough adjusted to their "hosts", to make a fair try at human behavior.

"I'll return it as soon as I can," Tom told the car's reluctant owner. Meanwhile, anybody can drive you home—anybody we've cleared." (I was keeping the "probable" mostly to myself—naturally. Nothing —death, volcanic eruptions, large green things with teeth—nothing causes panic like uncertainty. Human beings are not built for it, as a rule. For the most part, I kept the uncertainty under my own scalp, where, if I were going to get any good out of the human population at all, it belonged.) "And you won't be going anywhere for a while, now, will you?"

"But suppose I need——"

"If you need a car, your nearest neighbor can provide transport. And *will*, if it's that kind of emergency." Tom sounded as sure as if he'd given the neighbor orders himself.

He got the car keys.

And we drove home, without serious incident. I don't count the guy who came at me barrelling down the wrong side of the road at ninety miles an hour, and after he'd missed us chased us for six miles. That was no more than expected. Clearly the Somethings had a special category they'd put Gerald Knave in; as I say, a lot of the colonists seemed to know my reputation (damn it, I would *have* to start lying on those application forms! Beekeeper? Solipsist?); and, equally apparently, whatever the human beings knew, the Somethings knew when they took over.

So they had to figure I'd be the automatic leader of any attack on them. Maybe the Governor would be a danger—but they'd taken care of him. I was a prime target, and they knew it. Hell, if they hadn't known it before, the speech at the hospital would have told them.

Therefore: get rid of Knave. I could appreciate their reasoning. I wasn't really fond of them carrying it into action, but you can't have everything. And one guy in a car, not so good a driver as I happen to be, was no more than a small annoyance.

(Six miles is not the distance from the hospital to my place. It includes a lot of ducking down back roads, double-right-reverse turns, and other little items. Last time I saw the guy or the car he was in a large hay-bale, and in no condition for further chasing around. I had made a corner he'd thought he could make.)

My garage has a side door that opens right into the house. I got out of the car, watched Tom get out on his side—unfolding like a red-headed slide-rule—and went to that side door: why expose yourself to the uncertainties of the outside world?

36

Tom was on the other side of the car; I'd moved fast. I opened the door.

A laser beam came straight through it.

I heard Tom drop flat. Maybe he'd been hit, but I didn't think so: the garage smelled of burning aluminex, which is the stuff they use as the bottom trim on our ground-cars out here. (We're very fashionable, as colonies go. We could always afford to be.) The shot must have gone low, I thought—well, the door was one step up from the garage, and anybody standing on the other side had to shoot a little low to hit me in the body, the easiest fatal target. He'd shot a little too low, that was all, and the worst Tom had got, as far as I could figure, was a hot-foot.

Not that I was worrying about Tom then. I noted the fact and filed it, but I was in motion. I'd been in motion since I opened the door—I hadn't expected a laser, but I'd sure as Hell expected something, and taken steps not to be there when it arrived. Sure, I lock up; but windows are breakable, and even back doors have a regrettable tendency to yield to enough force or enough skill. If I were a prime target, then somebody would be planted waiting for me.

So I opened the door, went with its swingaway to the right, and was flat against the side wall watching the beam go by.

Then there was a short silence.

Little Something, what now?

How would he figure me? To stay and wait until he came out to get me? To come in low and fast? To try firing back?

I figured he would think of them all and wait a little

bit to see which checked out. So I gave him his answer: I leaned outward for a second and fired at a sharp angle into the open doorway.

I didn't hope to hit anybody—and I didn't. But that handgun of mine is a terror weapon. It isn't a nice hissing beam: it makes *noise*. And it fires a solid slug that chews up a lot of whatever it hits—in this case, a wall-corner in my kitchen. Maybe the colony would pay for repairs, when I got things cleaned out.

So I didn't wait. As I fired I was in motion. I came through the door behind the shot, at the same angle, low and fast. It had to take him a second to react, human or alien. And then he was likely to react without thinking.

Of course, if I'd underestimated the power of these alien things to adjust and reassess a situation . . . but I had the fight to go on. As I hit the doorway his second shot came—high this time, and away out to my left. I heard Tom curse.

Good: that meant he wasn't badly hurt.

And I had my man located. I kept moving. He was swinging the laser job up for a third shot—pretty fast, not more than half a second—when I had him. I fired without stopping to aim, still in my crouch and still going forward. Zigzag is a better defense tactic, but there was no damn time for defense.

I got him through the ear, believe it or not—creased his damn earlobe. A lot of good that did me.

Well, as a matter of fact, it did. I tell you, solid shot from a gun that size has a good deal of power. He was only grazed, but he rocked back, totally off-balance. He fired once straight into the ceiling; my bedroom was up there, and that determined me to make the colony pay for repairs, it was one great bedroom. Before he found his feet again I smashed his hand, the one holding the laser.

Then I got up close and used the butt of the gun on the side of his head. He dropped like a stone—not dead, just peacefully gone into dreamland, or wherever telepathic aliens go when out cold.

Gun battles are noisy, especially mine. The silence was a shock. I let it stand for a second or two before I said: "Tom? You okay?"

He was on the ground behind the car, hadn't even moved. The good, smart thing to do; the only way he could have helped me was by providing a naked target, and that's a little too much like suicide for any good man. He was fast; he could drop the guy if I didn't, once I'd either fallen or got into the house out of any possible line-of-fire—given that he was carrying a weapon, it occurred to me, which he probably wasn't. I keep forgetting that people will not be sensible about things like that; away back on Earth, in the middle of the Twentieth Century, there was a general feeling that guns killed people, and that the government should therefore take them away from the hands of law-abiding citizens, to avoid temptation and accident.

The notion had been tried in one of their large cities for years (see Sullivan Law: New York in any comprehensive encyclopaedia) and it had worked about as well as you might think—the honest citizens were un-armed, and the thieves and the killers, who regrettably had little respect for the law, had no strong opposition. The crime rate kept right on rising.

This fact stopped nobody from begging for a gun law that would cover all honest citizens, everywhere. It is not a subject on which people are sensible.

I go armed—which, on a colony world, is the only sensible thing to do. It draws stares, most places. Daddy, why is that man carrying that wicked gun?

Because he wants to reclaim its soul and turn it into a good gun, Sonny—by shooting some unlawful gunman with it. But try explaining that. You try it; I gave up years ago.

Tom wouldn't be armed, then.

All right; I could take care of that. "We're clear," I said. "At any rate, I think we are. This may have been a double setup; let me go through the house."

I did, with my gun in my hand. It holds ten shots; I had a plenty left for any character who popped up.

Nobody did. Conservation of energy, I supposed: if one man won't do the job, scrub it and wait for another chance.

There was something else about the setup that bothered me, but I didn't think of it then. I went back to the kitchen-garage door and called: "Are you hurt?"

"Not a scratch," he said. He'd been too shocked to find his voice, before. He moved fast; sometimes he reacted a little more slowly.

Well, I could take care of that, too, if I had the time. And I might need to.

"Come on in," I said. "We're clear."

He got up, dusty and white-looking. I shut the kitchen door behind us.

He leaned against it. I said: "Work first, relax later. Let's immobilize this character."

We did, with a dishtowel and a dustrag for ropes. Strong enough for immediate purposes. Tom said: "What did you want me here for?"

"Talk," I said. "We've got to have some names. Let's check out a few—now that we're all nice and safe and cozy."

He jerked a thumb at the man tied on the floor. "He'll hear," he said. "And—if they're telepathic, he'll pass it on to everybody in the network."

True: why give away information? Damn it, maybe I had been a little shaken. Nobody really likes being shot at. "Put him in a closet," I said. "Broom closet will do. We'll talk over by the 3V corner, with some nice loud tapes between."

"But maybe he can read our minds . . ."

"No chance." If any of them could have read our minds, we'd all have been dead; it's what you might call an unfair advantage in any fight like the ones we'd been through. No: for whatever reason, we were absolutely stone-cold immune to them.

Or did they just want us to think so?

That didn't make sense . . . or I couldn't see the sense it made.

Well, we could talk it over.

"I doubt they can," I said. "But if they can, it doesn't matter where we talk, or when. Might as well take standard precautions, and hope they work."

I put on an old one, the Shostakovich Tenth Symphony. It has passages as loud as any music I know, with the gain nicely cranked up.

And we talked.

VII

You may be noticing all these mentions of dish-towels and dustcloths and brooms. In this day and age? you may say to yourself.

I knew a gal once who flatly refused to believe I had any such equipment; had to take her up to my rooms, in the long run, and show her. It was a new switch: come up and see my whisk-broom?

But that was long ago, and on another planet . . . and so on. Why bother with it now?

In any case: in this day and age, yes.

Some people like to doodle. Some like to pace. Me, I like to cook, and wash, and clean. I'm a housewife —not by profession, but by avocation. I swear, I collect silver, all sorts of stuff, just for the fun of polishing it. I'd have made some ancient family a Hell of a good butler.

So I keep a Totum, for the days I don't really feel like indulging in my avocation—or the days I'm too damn busy, and that was one of them—and maybe a couple of other household Robbies. Spartan home. Wash and dry my own dishes. Bake about half of my own bread. Clean my own rugs and chairs.

Want to make something of it? Take it up with your favorite FemLib fanatic; I understand there's still a clot of them somewhere out by Alphacent. A group that denies facts of nature—sure, men and women are equal; what they're not is identical, in nature, aim or equipment—tends not to last very long, but the FemLib people have lasted longer than most. I think it may be because the thing got to be a religion, just preComity—around 2050. They've got a Pope (always by tradition named Joan), and a Chief Cardinal who claims direct descent from Mary Baker Eddy (which the Christian Scientists don't like, but the FemLibs have never worried about irritating people; it's the one thing I like about them), and a gallery of Saints. They've got their own St. Gloria, St. Betty the Ugly, St. Bella (or Ella; the records are confused) the Political—a whole roster. The whole thing began with somebody's joke about God being a female, and in the spate of religious revivals of that period some unknown founder said: "Why not?" and there they were. Most of them, as I say, are out by Alphacent, in a clot of their own, still working on parthenogenetics and depending on converts and the occasional "sin"—officially condemned, but unofficially forgiven instantly with a lot of talk about the Frailty of Woman that sounds like preComity Victorian England—to keep up their numbers. Give them another hundred and fifty years, they won't be there; they'll have gone to join the Holy Church of the Flat Earth, and similar sects. Denying reality is not a paying business for very long; any long-lasting religion has enough reality in it somewhere to stay alive on.

And what that has to do with the Cub IV situation. . . .

Well, never mind. So I do my own housework, and I keep a neat house, and it was a neat house Tom Pedon walked into, barring a bullet-hole in the kitchen corner-wall, a body on the floor (got some clean rags to bandage that hand and control the bleeding, and my Totum had sent out a Med call, of course; damn it, if I wanted to kill people I'd go and aim for the heart like everybody else) and—as suspected—a busted rear-living-room window. More for the colony to pay for, and I gave myself no better than a sixty-forty chance of getting the money. Gratitude is a wonderful thing—and it evaporates so fast!

We sat down in the 3V corner, well away from the busted window—well away from any window, or line of sight thereof—with Dmitri the Magnificent booming away on the audio speakers. Tom got himself my very best chair, real leather and maybe three hundred years old—what it costs in space-four shipment would make you cry, but I like a few indulgencies—and I drew a rocker up across from it, which was almost as good, maybe better. All the comforts of home. I reached over to a table at my right, next to the 3V cabinet, and opened a box on its top.

"Smoke?"

"Sure." Inoson tobacco, guaranteed danger-free. Sort of a cross between a short cigar and a long cigarette; I had mine dyed red on the wrapper, for no special reason except I liked it, and imported them by the giant's handful. Survival does pay off, now and then. Tom lit up and I lit up.

"They're not going to stop," I said. "Let's get that straight right now. They want us off this world, and they're going to keep up the pressure. Anybody they can take over——"

"And how many is that?" Tom said. "Half the world?"

It was a fair extrapolation from the hospital. "Maybe. Maybe a little less. But we've got to keep fighting back; and we'll need a group to do it with."

"Five people—six people—against half the planet?"

I took a long puff. "For a while, maybe. Not very long. I said we were going to be the leading edge, not the whole damn axe. If we begin to make a dent—we'll be joined."

He looked acutely uncomfortable. "Well . . . I don't know. . . ."

"I do," I said. "But it has to be the right people. We're going to have to make that dent."

"You mean—killing them? Killing the—people that have been taken over?"

"Not if we can help it," I said. "Immobilizing them. Defeating them and getting them out of the way." I took another puff. Inoson tobacco is lovely stuff. "Look, friend: we have no way of knowing that these takeovers are permanent."

He stared. "You mean they'll all get their minds——"

"Maybe," I said. "I don't know. Nobody knows—except the aliens, and they're not telling. Maybe the takeovers aren't spoiled for keeps." Privately, I thought that was a long chance; but it was one we had to take.

And I really don't even like killing aliens.

"But—they'll be trying to kill us," he said. The tobacco didn't seem to be soothing him any. Waste of a perfectly good, expensive tube. Hospitality is a depressing virtue. "They've already killed——"

"Haddison," I said. "Annal. Maybe more in the

45

hospital. They're two ahead of us at least; as far as I could see, we didn't cause a single fatality there.'' At the time, I didn't know what was happening to any of the others, on their ways home; well, I'd learn. But as far as I knew: ''We've killed nobody, unless the guy I shot in the shoulder decided to bleed to death despite medical attention.'' He'd gotten that, of course, as soon as everyone had left; I'd notified the appropriate staff.

''And if they try to kill us——''

''We'll try not to kill them,'' I said. ''You see why it has to be just the right group of people?''

The talk went on through four hours. The Med Robbies arrived and took my unsuccessful assassin away, under firm instructions not to let him loose; the Totum tidied up and brought coffee and a few bites while we balanced the names; Tom smoked six more of those cigarettes (which is what I call them; Inoson calls them Smoking Pleasure Tubes, Guaranteed Danger-Free and Delightful) and may have enjoyed one or two.

Let's summarize it. We ended up with four names.

Jimmy Dolin. Twenty-three years old, an arms hobbyist, fiercely independent—and not on bad terms with his parents. That last is a rare combination, and a good signal to look for, if you're hunting stability. Six feet one (taller than I am, by an inch), one hundred and forty-eight pounds (and twenty-seven pounds under my weight): a big yellow-haired stringbean who walked slow, talked slow, even looked at you slow—but who thought, and when he had to moved, at least as fast as Tom Pedon.

Elizabeth Storrs. Twenty-five, five-four, one

hundred and twenty-two pounds. Sanity is a tough quality to define; so is judgment. If I had to define either, I might just point the inquirer at Liz.

Harrison Mumm. Every group seems to need one total pessimist. I didn't especially start out to search for one, but we ended up with Harry because he was so damned competent. An electronics and molar-energy specialist, a family man of forty (whose family ran his wheat farm, and ran it damned well) vaguely interested in politics, deeply interested, now and then, in drinking. Five-nine, one hundred eighty, fair-to-middling with a gun—but show him a schematic for thirty seconds, and he will go away and build you several improvements. Tom thought we might need that sort of specialist, and so did I. But—well, put it this way. I know a couple of people who can get into deep dark moods, collect a lot of evidence and come to me with the absolutely certain news that the universe is due to end in forty minutes, there is no afterlife, and everything is useless and meaningless. Everybody knows one or two people like that—Hell, maybe everybody *is* one or two people like that, some of the time. But I only know one person who would come to me and give me that news—and enjoy doing it. What I mean when I say *pessimist.* Harry was the original.

Raythorne Wallis. A nice little old lady, Raythorne was—sweet and small and fragile to look at, and she dressed the part, by God. Maybe five-one, maybe ninety pounds. And the best surgeon and all-round medical expert on the planet.

She was the only one of the four we were reasonably sure of. None of the others had been at the hospital

—they weren't staff, they weren't sick, they hadn't been visiting (or, in Harry's case, called in to fix a sick mech). For all we knew, the other three might be aliens. In which case we would try again . . . but somehow I didn't think they would be. Whatever buried logic I was unable to locate in my head told me they were all okay.

And they were all people both of us knew, both of us could agree on. Jimmy, Liz, Harry, Raythorne: with us, six people, four men and two women.

If they were still human . . . I didn't think there was much chance they'd turn us down.

So—after four hours, when we had got down to that basic list—I punched the button for my Totum, and told him to start making phone connections, one at a time. Starting, I said, with Harry—might as well get the hopelessness out of the way to begin with.

And then Raythorne (at the hospital; but a call from me would pull her out of any but the most pressing emergency), Jimmy and Elizabeth.

I left the sanity, the way a child leaves the dessert, for last. That way I knew I could enjoy it more.

And she might have had some notions on substitute names, if any of the list had been—unavailable.

We were running lucky—or my subconscious was right. Or both.

We got all four.

The meeting—Meeting One, Guerrilla Force, Cub IV Colonization War—was set for eleven at night. My place.

And it was time for me to relax, by God. I left Tom with the 3V, the cigarettes, the tapes and a pile of microbooks. Me, I took my Totum in tow—I was going to need a little slavey-type help—and headed back to the kitchen . . .

I was going to cook up one Hell of a late supper for a guerrilla party.

VIII

It figured I was going to depend on the group when I had to, and go on my own whenever I could. Simple sense: one man is a lot tougher target to hit than six.

All the same, I needed the group now and then. Harry, for instance, came in handy right away; I had to know how to build a full communications network out of the phone setup on Cub IV.

It was the standard private-phone arrangement, with a single central switching system. What I wanted was a gimmick that would let me call up the whole human population at once—in our town, scattered outside, in the two tiny settlements that had just begun to grow —and let any of them get in touch with me instantly, wherever I was. "What you want is a radio system," Jimmy told me. "Give everybody portable receivers—Hell, maybe forty percent of the population has 'em now, they do music and Comity news and voice dramas that come in through space-four, and people like to take the radio out into the field, or maybe even into the store or the office."

"Sure," I said. "And in order to talk to everybody I have to be at the transmitting station—which strikes me, offhand, as one Hell of a dangerous place to hang around. Too many chances to get yourself neatly electrocuted. And anybody who wants to get in touch with me has to be at the transmitting station——''

''Talk band,'' Jimmy said. ''Use one band as a walkie-talkie special, and get everybody tuned to it——''

''Sure,'' I said. ''All the time. And if somebody joggles the knob or just plain decides he wants to find out what the Comity's doing, he's out of the net. Besides, I wasn't asking you.''

''Sorry I spoke.'' Jimmy was a little touchy. I guess we all were—except Liz. Seems to me, and I may be prejudiced, most capable people are touchy people. Show me a human being who's as calm and slow to anger as a clam, and I'll show you—a clam.

There are, of course, exceptions. Not very damn many, but Liz was one. If the human race were sane, everybody would act like Liz, more or less; and I'm afraid life would be much less interesting to me.

''We've got to get these things done right away,'' she told Jimmy. ''You were chosen—we five people were chosen—by Knave out of the entire planetary population.''

''Sure,'' Jimmy said sullenly. ''Big deal.''

''We're Knave's best picks for survival—we're the elite corps.'' Liz poured herself some coffee and filled Jimmy's cup again. My Totum, with a smaller Robbie as under-slavey, was washing up and putting things back where they belonged; the party had come to the coffee-brandy-and-cigars stage.

For which read coffee, and Inoson cigarettes. No

cigars because there weren't any cigars, and no brandy because I didn't want to start Harry off. Most times, he could take it or leave it alone. Once in a while, he didn't take it at all, it took him. I had no intention of trying to find out which sort of time we were in.

"Elite corps," Jimmy said, sounding no friendlier. Harry had a pad and a stylo out of his pockets, and was sketching something and occasionally saying: "Hmm," to himself in a worried sort of way.

"Well, we are," Liz said. "And, Jimmy—you don't mind if I call you Jimmy? We've barely met——"

"Sure," the kid said. "Jimmy. Fine with me."

"Your special talents are going to be needed," Liz said. "Knave thinks he can get the help he needs from you, Jimmy; from your own particular talents."

Jimmy sipped at the coffee. I make good coffee. The trick is, add a little salt to the ground beans before the water hits. "What talent?"

Liz looked surprised. "I have no idea," she said. "To be frank, I have no idea what my own—talent—is supposed to be." She sighed. "Of course, some of us are here for obvious reasons." She made being obvious sound like something no right-thinking person would really want to bother with. "Harry's electronics, for instance."

"Sure," Jimmy said.

"So for that sort of question, you see, Knave has to go to Harry. For other things, he'll have to come to—one of us. Me, perhaps. Or you. For the thing you can do best."

It was fairly primitive, but it smoothed the feathers

down nicely. Raythorne was sitting at her ease in my rocker, sipping and smoking, and Harry was still scribbling away. Liz had settled Jimmy down, and Tom was pacing the room, looking fairly relaxed for Tom. Whatever it was I had—guerrilla band, group therapy, sewing circle—we were all ready for work.

Liz gave me a quick look over Jimmy's head, and I looked back. She knew her special talent, all right. My look told her I did, too.

"You'd have to get into Central Exchange to work it," Harry said, coming out of his trance.

"What equipment, how long, and what are the side-effects?" I said.

Harry blinked at me mournfully. "Side-effects?" he said. "Oh—you mean what will this do to the telephone circuits. Nothing, of course; that was inherent in the problem. We'll still need normal phone service. That's a basic."

"Right," I said. "So?"

"I could do it with—oh, two people to help me," he said slowly. "They wouldn't have to know much. I mean, I wouldn't need electronics people especially. I could build most of the circuit right here, and it shouldn't take more than an hour to hook it up to Exchange. But we will have to get into Exchange."

"Is that so tough?" I said.

"They're very strict," Harry said. "IDs and badges and everything. Of course, I could probably send in a form for clearance and get an answer in——"

"The Hell with the form," I said. "We are now in a red-tape shortage period. I'll arrange it. How long to build the thing, and what will you need?"

It came to thirteen or fourteen hours, and a list of parts and wiring and oddments as long as your arm. Georgio Factor would have everything in stock, Harry was pretty sure. "That is, of course, if he's there. And if he hasn't—been taken over. If he has—well, then, I just don't know what we'll do." He looked normal, for Harry: totally hopeless. Even the meal hadn't cheered him up, but I didn't take that personally. You couldn't, with Harry. He made it so clear that you were only the smallest item in his world of disasters.

"We'll stage a raid—me and Tom and Jimmy—" The kid looked up at that, ready and then some—"and grab the stuff off the shelves." I got up and went for the phone. "First of all, we'll find out where we stand."

I dialled Georgio's place.

Nobody answered.

"We'll wait ten minutes," I said. "If we don't get an answer then, we go."

Liz looked at me. "Is this communications network so vital, right this minute?"

"Has to be," I said. "Damn it, I can't call up every person on Cub IV individually—and they're waiting on me for instructions."

"They probably have their radios on, or the 3Vs," Raythorne said.

"And if I have to raid something," I said, "I'd rather a small parts store than the communications complex. As it is, we're going to have to hold the Exchange until Harry's done, once we get in. Why go twice?"

"Right." She nodded and took in some coffee.

Ten minutes went by like years. I picked up the

phone again. Georgio hadn't been at the hospital, and he slept over his store; if he'd been home during the day, he probably hadn't been attacked—physically. What shape his mind was in, I didn't know.

He answered on the fifth ring. "Huh?"

He'd been sleeping. "Georgio? Gerald Knave. Go down and open the shop right away—no, in ten minutes. We'll be down there to—"

"Knave?" he said foggily. "Do you have any idea what time it is?"

"What the Hell difference does that make?" I said, and then I blinked. Sure enough, there were still people like Georgio—people who just hadn't happened to be anywhere where any fight at all had gone on, and hadn't heard from friends. Georgio had no notion there were aliens invading minds all over Cub IV; for him, it had been a perfectly normal day and, until I pulled him out of it, a perfectly ordinary night's sleep.

I filled him in, in a hurry.

Naturally, he didn't believe me. Maybe he thought he was still dreaming; it must have sounded like one of your choicer wild nightmares.

Liz took the phone. She was the convincer.

"All right," I said when she'd put it down. "We have ten minutes. I'm going out with Tom and Jimmy. Harry, you'll have to come along."

"I will?" he said. He looked even more mournful.

"Unless you can give me a list that tells Georgio *exactly* what you need, no substitutes and no questions. Nobody else can recognize enough of the stuff to clear it."

"The list you have should do," he said. He held up a

hand. "No, wait a minute," he said, took the list off the table where it was lying, and added at the bottom: "Can use 3N3V4 circuit for one 44BB, but need all else as stated."

He handed it to me and I took it.

Jimmy said: "But Georgio was okay. You're taking a—raiding party anyhow. Why?"

"Because," I said, as gently as possible, "we're going to have to get there, and get back. And stand around while Georgio picks all this stuff off his shelves. And load it into the car. And during every second of that time, we are going to be targets."

"Oh," Jimmy said.

"From now on," I said, "think of yourself as a target—anywhere, doing anything. You'll be seen with me, one way or another; you may have been traced here tonight."

"My goodness," Raythorne said.

"I'm serious," I told her. She didn't look alarmed. I'm told she never did, even in the Operating Theater when Rance Johannsen had a heart attack in the middle of the gallstone removal. She didn't look the slightest bit surprised or off-balance, and she never stopped. Rance recovered. "These Somethings—they don't seem to have a name; we'll have to give them one when we find time—they're after me; you all know that."

"You're our expert," Liz said.

"In survival," I said, and tossed her back her own ball; "I need the rest of you for your own specialties." I looked around, taking in everyone. "They're going to be aiming at me—but if I'm not available, any one of you would be a fine consolation prize."

55

"I see," Raythorne murmured. She stubbed out a cigarette.

"They know you're on this team," I said. "And if they can damage the team, they will. Every human being on Cub IV is a target, and has been since Laia Kodorko this afternoon; but you five might mean a little more to them. Bigger point-score."

"Okay," Jimmy said. He was on his feet. "Okay. So let's go. We only got ten minutes, right?"

"Right," I said, and we moved.

IX

The strange thing is, we got there without any trouble at all.

I had the list in my left-hand pocket. I was carrying my gun in my right hand. Tom was on my right, Jimmy on my left. They were both armed; I'd outfitted them from personal stores. I knew Jimmy could shoot; I was a little afraid Tom would blow his foot off or something, but maybe he was good and I'd never known about it.

The store had its lights on: a nice little two-story place, all set up prefab by the Robbies along a side street. Alley on either side; we're not crowded for land. Lights on upstairs and down, and a jumble of parts and radios and such in the windows; door in the center, shade pulled down but light sneaking around it. I pushed the bell. Inside there was a nice little bong. A second went by.

Then a laser beam came straight through the door.

That had been the long chance. Tom and Jimmy were to the sides; I damn near knocked Tom over moving out of the way. At that I got a small scorch on my sleeve, but I didn't notice any pain then.

I hadn't figured the long chance, not really. Apparently the back of my head was smarter than the front —something I'd known all along; if we had to depend on what we *knew* we knew, we'd all have been dead at age six. It had set up a reflex, and with the first faint hiss of the beam, before the door was holed through, I'd moved.

"Georgio?" I called. Maybe, just maybe, somebody had got to his place after the call, taken care of Georgio and waited in the place for me. It wasn't impossible —not quite. Of course, they'd have to have known I was coming there, but there were any number of ways to figure that out. Hell, if I could figure my own best move, so could they; and Harry's trip to my house could have been seen easily enough.

But something bothered me, something else . . .

The back of my head is smarter than the front: sure. So why doesn't it give lessons? I had a good deal of stuff back there I would have paid real money to have in the front of my head, where I could get at it. Instead, I was just going to have to wait.

That is, if I lived to get it.

A voice said: "I am Georgio. We are here." It was the same voice I'd been hearing: not human. Not at all. Another beam came through, this one aimed nicely, by ear, at where I'd been standing.

I wasn't there; I was around the side of the place, in the alleyway, dragging Tom along. I'd given Jimmy a signal to take the other side, and I hoped he'd got it; I hadn't waited to see.

He was a good kid, though, when he had to be: right on schedule. I heard the crash of glass as a window broke on the other side, and then the hiss of the beam. I only hoped he'd had sense enough to toss his stone, or whatever, and get the Hell down fast. Meanwhile, Georgio's mind (or whatever mind was using Georgio) was distracted for a second. I was at the window on our side. I shot through it once in the general direction of the other window, and then went through rolling.

The beam went over me. Tom yelled. Flesh wound—maybe.

But it located Georgio for me; the lights were out by then. He'd cut them with the first beam. It was the right move; whatever you could say about these Somethings (and I found I could say a great deal, if I had the time for it), you couldn't call them stupid.

I wondered (even then) if they'd ever run into another race. I even felt sorry (though, as it turned out, I didn't really have to) for the other race.

And I wondered who was going to feel sorry for us? For the poor, damned, stubborn human race, finally facing an enemy it couldn't understand, and maybe couldn't out-think?

Georgio was near the center of the room. I let a shot go in that general direction; I wasn't aiming—Hell, I hadn't even got to picking splinters out of my clothes and hair from the window-plastic.

Expert shooting. He yelled and I heard a clunk; by God, I'd hit him in the gun arm. I hit him again for good measure, trying not to kill him, and he went down all at once. Georgio had been one big man; almost anybody would have gone down with the first slug.

I searched round the walls for lights, slightly conscious of possible booby-traps but not really believing in them. I found the lights and switched them on. The place was a mess. My Totum is efficient, and it might have taken him, and me, working together, two days to clean the room up. First, of course, there was the body . . .

I found a phone and put in a quick call to my place. Liz answered the phone. I told her to bring the others, and fast: I needed Harry, now, to identify the stuff on his list, and I needed Raythorne for Georgio. No sense letting him bleed to death all over his own good floor.

Tom climbed in then, and Jimmy busted his own window—a waste; when the kid didn't absolutely *have* to think, he didn't bother with it—and joined the happy crew. I began to realize just how lucky I was being. Damn it, I had to wind things up before my string ran out and I really did get beamed.

Which reminded me of my arm, which began to hurt like Hell. I spent most of the time until Raythorne got there trying for something really special in the way of cursing.

It's not something I'm terribly good at. Raythorne just looked at me, when they'd all arrived and I was winding up with some fancy flourishes, and said: "Tsk."

For cursing, that's a total pan review.

She got to work on Georgio at once—I'd tied him but

left one arm more or less free for her. He wasn't about to harm her with it; two slugs had just about put it out of commission permanently. She hummed while she worked, I noticed, not a tune I could identify. The way Harry hummed while he sketched diagrams.

I began to wonder if I hummed while I was shooting. I discovered it was something I'd never know; how would I ask anybody?

Liz told me she'd done the driving, as I'd asked. If you have sanity on call, use it—one more good rule. We talked for a while. Harry was at the shelves and the bins, humming and taking out one weird thing after another. Jimmy was just standing around, and Tom—my God, I'd forgotten him.

He was leaning against the wall, near the window we'd come in. At first I couldn't see a wound anywhere; he was wearing dark stuff, and beams don't generally make for blood. "Where did he get you?" I said

"Hip."

I looked and found it, a good burn. I called to Raythorne, and she looked up. A nice little old lady interrupted at her knitting.

"Just a second now, Jerry." I think she was the only one who called me Jerry all the time. Jimmy tried it, and so did Tom, but mostly everybody settled for Knave.

Unimportant details, file under.

"Tom over here," I said. "Hip burn. Georgio's laser."

"Not Georgio," Tom said. "Georgio'd never—it's that thing. Them things."

"Sure."

Harry was building a nice pile, half on the counter and half on the floor. I was glad I'd asked for everybody—Hell, I'd had to—because Jimmy, half of Tom, and an unknown percentage of me would never have got all that to the car, even with Georgio helping.

Damn it, I remembered Georgio. He'd helped rig my audio setup. A cheerful bald man with an unending thirst for good beer, and the paunch to prove it.

Georgio had no business being—an alien.

Not Georgio. Not anybody I knew.

I realized I was beginning to get angry at them, for the first time. I looked at that for a second, and damn near started laughing as Raythorne straightened up and came over to take a look at Tom. On the way she said to me: "You take things easy, too. I want to see that burn."

"Don't bother with it," I said. What the Hell was I turning into, a hero? "On second thought, bother with it. Your very best bothering."

Raythorne gave me an absent smile; she was already concentrating on Tom's wound. That took her ten minutes and a fair amount of salve and bandage out of her bag. Mine took five, and less. And why had she brought the bag?

Sure. Because I'd told her to. Me, Knave, who thinks of everything.

I wish I had. But I'd dropped that little detail—damn it, getting shot at was definitely beginning to upset me. It had been Liz who'd made the suggestion.

Well, it's what I said. If you have sanity around . . .

Among us all, we got Harry's pile to the cars. Raythorne didn't try to keep me from driving one of them back home. Maybe she knew she couldn't. Maybe, on the other hand, I just wasn't wounded that badly. My luck, so to speak, was holding.

I wondered how much more of it I'd have.

X

Surprise: we got home without losing anybody, without wrecking any cars, and with the entire pile of Harry's equipment intact.

My luck, if that's what it was, was holding. True, we'd been shot at three times, from various windows; but it takes a fair shot to hit a moving car with a beam (or a slug, for that matter), and it takes a good powerful gun to do anything more than scratch the outside of the car slightly.

Into the garage with both cars (the place was roomy enough; we had room to spare, on a first-generation colonization planet), and nobody opened a door except Yours Truly, Survivor, damn it all. Nobody else to take the damn risks. I came out into the open air and waited for a beam or a slug. Nothing happened.

Maybe there was a welcoming committee inside the house, I thought. It would just have to wait; there was nothing we could do about it from the garage.

I signalled the others, and everybody piled out. I made myself a rule: Never leave home without setting someone on watch, and someone you can trust. I mean, this tiptoe stuff every time I came back to my own peaceful house could get a little wearing.

That night, though, there'd been nobody to leave.

So we went in carefully. Swing a door open, stay out of the way, and wait. Walk in—or run in—at an angle, low. Light every light you can find.

·And cover every room.

We did; and we found nobody. I told myself that the Somethings undoubtedly had other things to do; they couldn't spend their whole time just on me. But you know, it made me feel neglected. For a change, nobody was trying to kill me.

Harry went back to the garage, where we had left the pile. One of the things I do not want is a lot of electronic workshop gunk all over my nice neat living room. The Totum might be able to clean most of it up; but Harry could work in the garage just as well, and come into the house (suitably washed) for meals. Why not arrange it the simple way?

Raythorne checked me and Tom, made a few adjustments in bandaging, and went off to bed—first upstairs guest-room. Jimmy and Tom had a brief argument with me about setting a watch, which I won, and they went off—second guest-room. Liz was bedded down with Raythorne, no argument at all. Sex, or love, or the Life Force, or whatever it is you happen to call it, just had not had time to raise its teeny head.

I sat in the living room, instructed the Totum to spread its eyes and ears to its under-slavies, my two Robbies, and tell me instantly of anything unusual —and had to spend ten minutes defining "unusual": have you ever tried it, even with a good Totum?

I also asked him to bring me coffee, if there was any left.

Compliment to my householder's abilities: I had to go and make a fresh pot.

Well, it took up some time.

And when I had the coffee and a cigarette to hand, I took one deep breath and did the only sensible thing. I got on the phone.

When Harry was finished, and we'd gotten his gimmick attached to the main exchange, we'd know it all; we'd be in contact with everybody. But that was going to take time, and it was full of ifs; meanwhile, I could tap a few people, here and there, and find out just what sort of thing was actually happening.

I spent five hours on the phone. I woke some people, not many; a lot seemed to be keeping an all-night watch, splitting time with their wives or husbands or children. (Totums are not very good at that sort of thing. For one thing, you have to define "unusual": for another, they will not harm human beings. And a Something would be a human being, to a Totum. Waking a human to take care of the unusual event would be time-consuming; and time, everybody did seem to realize, we didn't have. No: watches were kept by humans. Or what I was fairly sure were humans.)

And I suppose I could give you the word-for-word data on every damn call. I'm a basically nice guy; I'll do it the way the Comity news people do it when they beam their dailies out this way in space-four. Like so:

Item: of the four Reagans, three had got home, and none without injury; they were on pain pills and home bandages and such. Seems Carlion Lindorenyko had not been immune.

The Lindorenykos were noted for their size and strength. Carlion—or what had been Carlion—had just picked up the car the Reagans were driving home in and flipped it straight backward. They'd stopped at his signal, thinking maybe he'd been stranded and needed help.

The car had actually turned over twice, by some freak, and landed right-side-up; and before Carlion could get to it the Reagans were away. But they'd been thoroughly shaken up, and there seemed to be a broken bone or two in among the list of casualties.

Item: Carol Dennis wasn't answering the phone. Her sister Freida was; but Freida had been taken over. The voice wasn't one I was likely to mistake. I asked her where Carol was. She only said that we all were going to leave, and they could not be resisted. I thought I heard some sounds deep in the background, but I couldn't be sure; and after the third go-round on the Somethings not being resisted I hung up. Note the Dennis household for action, as soon as possible.

Item: some damn fool—human or otherwise—had set fire to the Graumann house. I got the details from the Fredericks family, who worked the next farm; the Graumann place was burning merrily as they watched. Two of the Fredericks boys had gone out to see if they could be any help—commendable reflexes, but not showing a great deal of sense, under the circumstances. Mrs. Fredericks was beginning to break under the strain; the boys had gone two hours before and she'd had no word. Gene Fredericks said they'd be back, sure, trying to sound as confident as all blazes. I remembered they had a daughter, Dorene. I asked about her. Gene said: "Forget it. We're not—worrying about Dorene any more." So I knew what had happened there.

Item . . . but a few samples are enough. I got five hours of it, and the net totals looked pretty clear. The human race was losing. My original guess figures seemed to be about right: nearly half of the population had been taken over, and the other half seemed to be wholly immune. (Was there something in that to work on? I filed it. What did we have in common, the ones who were still human?) It should have been an even battle—maybe. Hell, we seemed to have a slight edge in the numbers: why weren't we ahead?

Trouble is, most human beings are like me in one very important respect.

They don't like to kill.

Oh, they will, given enough reason for it, and given enough training—and there are always the maniacs, the ones who've got too damned much reason-for-killing filling their heads (the little green men told them to; that sort of thing) or the ones who don't need any reason at all, the ones who kill because it's convenient. And there are the very, very few who really like it.

It's a bell curve, more or less—talk to an analytic psychologist for the figures, if there are any, and I'm sure there are; those people have figures for everything—with the total pacifists at one end, the ones who simply will not kill under any circumstances whatever, and the ones who find killing fun at the other end, both terribly small minorities.

In between is the human race.

And the human race needs a fairly strong reason for killing. Just like me; I think in that area I'm somewhere near average.

God knows the aliens were reason enough, when you saw one coming at you, when you heard one telling you he couldn't be stopped and he was going to stop *you*. . . .

But reasons take time to be believed, thought out, and acted on. That alien looks exactly like your Aunt Winifred, which adds to the delay. A human being needs time to decide to kill; he needs a little more time to decide to kill something he knows is an alien, but sees as a human being he's grown up with.

And the aliens needed no time at all.

They knew what they were doing: they were ridding the planet of its pests.

They had the jump on us from the start, and they weren't about to lose that advantage.

The Reagans stopped for Carlion Lindorenyko. Two Fredericks boys—with an example in their own family!—had gone out to help the Graumanns.

That sort of thing was their advantage.

Five hours of phoning told me they were making the best possible use of it.

We were behind. And unless I could find a whole lot of rabbits to pull out of some hats I was going to have to find somewhere, we were going to stay behind.

Until, of course, we just weren't around any more.

XI

I slept some. So did everybody else except Harry. He didn't seem bothered by staying awake for sixteen hours or so—a lot more, come to think of it; I never did ask him when he'd slept last. He looked a little more mournful, maybe, but that was about it.

Apparently, with a nice problem to work on, he didn't need sleep. But the rest of us did.

And the night went by, and the morning. Early afternoon, we were all awake, and milling around the house. I'd filled the rest in on my phone checks, and nobody was anxious to do many more. Raythorne had to call the hospital—Tom had to call Tobor Raisford —Jimmy had to call his folks (I told him I'd already done that, which was true, and that they were all okay—which might have been true. The parents sounded human, but Jimmy had a two-year-old sister. Would the aliens take over a two-year-old child? And how would you tell, for sure, if they did?) . . . only Liz had no calls to make.

They used the phone. Raythorne got a progress report, which was good news, for a change—apparently that first battle had tipped the balance out there, and human beings were still in control. The emergency wards were full-staffed with every available attendant as well as the doctors and mechs, and all armed with needles full of sleepy stuff. That situation sounded as if it would stay solid: doctors have a faster reaction time than the general populace anyhow, and a lot less resistance to overcome when they know they're just putting somebody harmlessly to sleep, not killing him.

The hospital was human-controlled. It was busy; Raythorne quite obviously thought about going back there, and decided the team needed her more where she was. But it was, more or less, running.

Tobor Raisford's phone didn't answer.

We knew Tobor was immune (or we thought we did). I didn't have any soothing words to offer. Tom looked a little blank, and then settled down to wait. He kept rubbing the stock of the rifle I'd given him.

Jimmy did call his folks; well, you couldn't really expect second-hand reassurance to satisfy him. Apparently the call went off peacefully. He came back looking almost relaxed, until he got a glance at Tom's face.

Early afternoon: Harry came up out of the garage and tramped into the living-room. He looked around at us. "Got it," he said. "If you think it's going to do any good, it's all ready."

"Now, all we have to do is hook it in," I said. "Right?"

"If you think we can get into the Exchange," Harry said. "But they must be guarding——"

"Leave that to me," I said. Harry was off on a flight of depression; I didn't need him spreading the gloom around.

Tom's face was doing enough of that. Liz had gone over to his chair to talk to him, but there had been no result. Whatever he was feeling wouldn't dent or melt; and that's the way his face looked.

More than that, we distinctly did not need.

Reasons for working alone . . . you know how long a list that is, when you sit down and think about it?

But for the moment . . .

Harry was looking at me with his eyebrows raised a little.

"I have a plan," I said.

Well, Hell. I had, if you want to know.

Maybe it would even work.

The Central Exchange was a building by itself, on a block by itself, three stories high (with no divisions between the stories—no real floors except at ground level, just walkways), without windows. There were four ground-level doors, one per side of this box, all of them leading to walkways inside that made the place a giant maze. There were elevators at every intersection and more walkways strung here and there from various units at what might have been second-floor level or third-floor level. It was like a three-dimensional chess setup, with every square filled with machinery: the walkways and elevators were the lines between the squares.

Harry's gimmick had to go up near the top, at a location he described as C3AA45. He said he could point it out to me.

If anybody was waiting for us—and I had to agree, it sounded like a sensible thing to do, guarding the Exchange, just on general principles—they had to be at the four doors.

So we weren't going in any of them.

We were going to make our own door.

There were four of us—the four men. Harry because somebody had to do the pointing, and if possible the attaching (he'd drilled Jimmy in the job as well as possible, just in case). Me because I was the local expert, and, such as it was, it was my plan. Jimmy because we needed a backup for Harry, and Jimmy was our fastest volunteer. And Tom because nobody could have left Tom sitting home staring at nothing with that face.

We took the Hell of a lot of equipment.

And we parked one block away from the Exchange building. That block had a two-story-high building on a corner near the Exchange. We got out of the car and walked around to the building, keeping it between us and any possible Exchange guards. We climbed a flight of stairs with all the damn equipment split up among the four of us, and got out onto the roof.

The building was a lumber-supply company, or what passed for it: not actual lumber, but plastic imitations, strong enough to use for building small additions to your house or farm. The company was closed down, but I know a little about locks, here and there. In a way, I was vaguely surprised the company even had locks; most private houses didn't.

What we needed was a good long slab of imitation wood, as strong and as light as possible.

It wasn't on the second floor.

Sure: it was on the ground floor. The staircase was a straight slope—if it had been a curve, I suppose we would have figured out something else, but that much luck we did have—and we snaked it up the slope, returning to the second floor to see it lying there with its

71

end at the far wall. The thing was better than sixteen feet—long enough, figuring a seven-foot rise between buildings and a thirteen-foot (by local statute) space for the street. Pythagoras gives you the answer: the seven-foot rise and the distance between buildings were the sides of a right-angle triangle; we were going traveling on the hypotenuse.

The lumber-supply building had an access door to the roof. I went up the ladder and propped it open and stood there, letting Tom and Jimmy do the heavy work of snaking the board around so it stuck up along the ladder and up past me into midair.

We snaked it out onto the roof. Harry came along last with the bag of equipment on a long rope.

And then we swung it around until it touched the Exchange building roof, one story higher up. Pythagoras had not let us down: it fit.

We were making very little noise.

I sent Tom and Jimmy down the ladder to get more plastic imitation stuff and they came back and weighted down our end of the bridge with it.

The other end just sat there, on the Exchange roof. Maybe it would shift, maybe not.

I took most of the equipment with me as a weight —strung out in a sling on that long rope straight behind me.

I went across. On my hands and knees.

The board seemed to have a tendency to sideslip. I kept feeling that the string of stuff behind me was going to catch on something, though there was nothing for it to catch on: that board was *smooth*.

I took it an inch at a time, feeling like the center ring at one of your better circuses.

Halfway across, a beam put a nice smoking hole in my board, six inches in front of my nose. Somebody back on the two-story let out a yell.

A guy on the ground, firing straight up. I didn't move; where the Hell was there to go? Another hole appeared, smoking, a foot ahead of me; the guy was shooting by guess, calculating where I had to be from the way the board bellied down. He was close—maybe he'd figured me to keep going, and was leading me —but he wasn't going to get any closer.

I hoped.

I swear I did the single slowest draw in the history of the human race.

He had time for a nice, careful third shot before I had my gun out. I should have had it in my hand right along—but that character was the one I never expected.

They do say it's the surprises that kill you.

His third shot nicked the edge of the board, still six inches off. At the rate he was going, two more shots would be enough even if he missed me: he'd have put enough holes in the board to snap it, and a two-and-a-half-story drop didn't sound healthy. Not that the drop mattered: there he'd be at the bottom, waiting to finish me off with one more little beam.

It seemed as if my luck had run out.

Maybe it took me thirty seconds to draw. I was trying to stay balanced all this time. I leaned slightly out toward my right and the damn board leaned with me. I heard the equipment string begin to slide, and stop as I pushed back.

The guy underneath was waiting. Somebody was still yelling over on the two-story, but I couldn't distinguish words.

Advice, maybe.

The street guy had all the time in the world. He had to see me shift and then pull back; now he was waiting for a good clear shot. I confused him a little, moving from side to side.

Good for me. As I got back to dead center, I leaned out again—damn quick. My gun was out further than my head. I pushed the gun arm down as I fired, to minimize recoil—with that job, it's considerable, and if I hadn't compensated it could have blown me backward right off the board.

I had to be a good shot.

Surprise: I am a good shot.

I'd caught him the first time I leaned over. The second time I didn't have to locate him; all I had to do was shoot where I'd already seen him. He wasn't going any more places than I was.

And I hit his right knee, believe it or not. He had one leg stuck out in front of him. I'd aimed for the shoulder or the head. I was off just enough to blow his knee to little pebbles.

He was lucky: he wasn't conscious long. There is no worse pain in the world, they tell me—ancient duellists used to try to kill most of their targets, but the ones they really hated got "starred" kneecaps. It may not kill you (though in the duelling days the state of medicine was such that I would not bet on it); but you wish it had.

Plain simple luck, his and mine.

Ant time running out. I took one deep breath and went on across the bridge. I made it to the other side without incident, and weighted it down with the equipment I pulled in behind me. Now it was more or less safe (though I would never have recommended it to your average pedestrian); it was anchored at both ends.

I was making hurry-up signs. The others made it one by one, just fast enough; a shot burned the board behind Harry as he stepped off onto the roof. We were standing on more of the same imitation stuff: it's not only strong; it's also nonconductive.

Down below, of course, there were now three guards, minimum, all waiting for us to get inside the building. My gun is noisy, but they hadn't needed that. Telepathic, remember?

I didn't envy the three conscious ones the memory of that knee.

What we had to begin with was a very tight beam and a set of metal prongs. I beamed two tiny holes in the roof—bursts fast enough so they just barely went through, and didn't damage God knows what equipment underneath—and stuck in the prongs. Then I beamed a large circle around the holes.

I was waiting for them to blow up the building.

Damn it, they were telepaths. What did they need Central Exchange for?

I filed the question. Tom had hold of the prongs. We all stood clear. He jerked the circle straight out.

All we had to do was drop down to a walkway maybe eight feet below us.

These walkways are fairly wide—made for man or Robbie, or even Totum. An eight-foot drop is perfectly reasonable.

And if they hadn't blown up the building, they were going to be damn careful about shooting us: a wild beam would ruin a lot of banks and exchanges.

I got down. Then Jimmy, then Harry. Tom lowered the sling full of equipment down to Harry, and waited while we all started off toward C3AA45. Then he came down.

He'd left the circle and prongs up on the roof someplace. He caught up with me a couple of feet down a walkway.

"Who the Hell was that?" he said, sounding winded.

I thought of the guy I'd shot. "I didn't stop for introductions."

"Maybe you should have," he said. "I've got a nice question for you."

"Shoot." It wasn't the right word. I winced a little.

Tom didn't wince. "Tell me this," he said. "How did anybody know you were going to be out there?"

It stopped me, but only for a second. "He didn't have to know. All he had to do was pass by and see the bridge. He wasn't shooting at me—but he'd know I wasn't part of the alien network, whoever I was. Maybe he was a guard who just happened to look up."

"Maybe," Tom said.

I didn't like it. We hadn't made a lot of noise. And people don't look up very much—it seems to be a habit that's been bred out of the human race. And the yelling hadn't started until after the first shot.

But Tom was right: "maybe" was the word.

I filed it.

It struck me that my files were getting a little crowded. I'd have to take some time off shortly, I told myself, to look them over.

And anyhow, who the Hell cared what I liked?

XII

All this took about ten seconds. The guards were still looking for a clear shot, and Harry was still looking for C3AA45. I'd got behind him and Jimmy and the sling, and they hit the intersection first.

That was the clear shot. I yelled: "Side!" and Jimmy pushed Harry across the intersection to the left, making less of a target by cutting the corner than by going on straight ahead. Jimmy went on right after him.

I hadn't reached the intersection when they hit him.

He went down—falling into the side passage, which saved his life. The beam had got him along one side, how seriously I couldn't tell. He'd straightened and then fallen flat, which did not look good.

The guard fired again as I came through. But I'd given him one straight down, and it upset him. He damn near hit a bank. I gave him another one while Tom cut the same corner.

Harry was kneeling down at Jimmy's head. I said: "How far?"

"Straight?" he said. "Back to the intersection, two banks." About twelve feet. No trouble, but we'd have to cross two more intersections on the way.

And Jimmy was out of it.

Tom said: "All right. Let's go."

"You and Harry," I said. "I'll stay here and keep them busy."

"What the——"

"Harry has to get his gimmick stuck on. We can't leave Jimmy. Maybe I can occupy the guys down below while you do the job, get back and tap into the lines to my place."

Harry blinked. "Tap into—you mean, call your phone? From here?"

I may have cursed a little. "Isn't that what this is all about?" I said. "Use your gimmick, and——"

"You can use any phone to tap into any other phone, or any combination," he said. "But——"

"Damn it, figure a way," I said. "Liz is going to have to get the Hell over here with a heli, and fast. I can just maybe keep them busy while you get your work done. I can't keep them busy while you go and hunt for a nice normal telephone down below somewhere. That way, we all go."

He shut his eyes.

There had been no shots from below. I figured them to do it the smart way: one guy under the intersection we'd just cornered by, one guy at the next one to the left—where Harry and Jimmy had headed—and one straight ahead, since I'd yelled: "Side." Which meant we hadn't been planning on a turn in the first place.

I went on to the left intersection and fired down. The banks cast weird shadows; I couldn't see anybody at all down there. If I hit anything, it didn't make a sound.

I scurried on back to the intersection we'd left. Harry and Tom and the sling came with me and went right on, toward the straight-ahead intersection, as I fired down again.

No sound.

Harry stopped before he got to the next intersection.

Tom was behind him, cradling the sling. I had room to sidle past both.

I had six shots left. I hoped I wouldn't need seven.

I fired down. Somebody yelled.

Score one.

"Now!" I said. "Fast!"

A guy gets hit, he's in shock. Not for long, maybe. You can measure it in seconds, and not many of them, if he's good.

But when one guard got hit—all three were in shock. Telepaths: remember?

We had those seconds.

I think we made a Cub IV record for the six-foot dash.

Harry got to work. Tom said: "Okay now. Suppose I go back and——"

"You stick here," I said. "I'm the expert, remember?"

I had a second thought, and borrowed the small rifle I'd given Harry. Tom was armed, with a bigger job; Harry wouldn't have a lot of time to use a weapon, and six shots—five shots, I corrected myself—looked smaller every second.

Then I made it back to Jimmy. Fast and quiet. By that time, there was no smart way for the guards to play it; we'd had enough time to get to any one of several intersections, and past them.

Quiet enough, I figured, and they wouldn't try beaming me. They wouldn't be shooting at random.

No, as it turned out, they wouldn't. The two of them who were still active were coming up the elevators after us.

I hoped to Hell Harry was hurrying. Once we were all on the same level of walkway, they didn't have to wait for intersections: the nice wide walkways gave them plenty of space for a clear shot.

Jimmy stirred a little. I put a hand over his mouth.

He bit it.

Unconscious spasm. Just not my day.

I didn't yell; silence was the whole idea.

I could hear the elevator whine. The building was full of echoes; I couldn't tell where it was. Ahead of me, behind me, to either side—my God, I thought, if they come up near Harry and Tom . . .

The whine stopped.

They were somewhere on our level.

Offhand, I gave us maybe one chance in four. Maybe a little less.

XIII

Maybe a lot less.

I'd been figuring two of them active, three of us (well, Harry was busy, and not much of a shot, and —call it two and a half; no, go ahead and call it two).

Why couldn't a group of telepaths call for nearby reinforcements?

Those elevators could fit five. If I'd only heard one (and I did think I could swear to that) it was any number from two to five against us.

When the shooting started I thought they'd got to Tom and Harry.

I didn't find out until later what had happened.

Harry explained it to me. Patiently. I was a small child who couldn't be expected to understand complex matters.

"Well, of course, if you said it had to be done then it had to be done," he told me. "And it was first priority—that was how you explained it."

That was how I'd explained it, all right.

"So I didn't bother wiring in the entire board," he said. "I took enough out to make a connection—bank to bank. You know it's possible to tap any line from any bank?"

I hadn't known that, no. There seemed to be a lot I hadn't known.

"Failsafes," Harry said. "And duplicate availables—so when a new phone is added, you don't have to rewire every existing bank to connect it to the other phones. You can connect it to any handy bank."

Well, well, I said.

"It's the only simple way," Harry said. "And bank-to-bank, I connected Central Exchange—that's the prime connection, easiest to snap on anywhere —with your phone."

I said: "How did you find my phone line? And how did you find something to talk through?"

Harry sighed. He was stuck with a slow learner. "Any individual line is a coded pulse," he said. "I had the power in the rig we'd brought in; I sent the pulse through the new connection: Central Exchange to your phone. What else?"

What else, indeed?

"And conversation—well, every bank has a speaker-and-headset combination," he went on. "To

check out malfunctions when you're working on repair.
Call the phone you're working on from whatever bank
you're working at.''

Simplicity itself. Why hadn't I thought of it?

(Well, I told myself, I would next time—in whatever
shape next time presented itself. It was new information; some day it might turn out valuable. A survivor is
an information collector.)

''The only hard part was getting to the headset,''
Harry said. ''I told Tom to cover me—of course that
setup is as near to the intersection as possible.''

Of course. And he'd made it, while I was being bit by
my temporary patient—and Liz had not wasted any
time.

The nearest heli was four houses away. Liz had put
Raythorne on the phone to the owners, grabbed her car,
and made it in seconds.

Heli to Exchange roof, more seconds.

And then down the hole we'd made—and pure dumb
luck. Instead of landing in front of the guards, she'd
landed five feet behind them.

She had a beam, and she took two shots. The day
may come when Liz will need more than one shot per
target, but it is going to be a very surprising day.

Harry went on working. Tom and Liz and I were
pretty busy, too, until he was done.

The guards had called for reinforcements, after all.

But they'd called for them on the ground, which gave
us time in the first place, and a fairly easy defense setup
in the second.

We split up—at once, almost before Liz's two vic-
tims had dropped—to cover three of the four doors.

Two of us—Liz and I—had line-of-sight back to the roof-hole, since we didn't know for sure we were going to be up against ground troops. We didn't even know for sure the reinforcement call had gone out; we just had to figure it that way.

It left one door uncovered. But that took even a telepathic net a little time to realize—and by then we were withdrawing from our positions. Liz had come down the hole by heli ladder; we went up the same way: Liz and Harry and Jimmy first load (to a roof two blocks off), with Liz cradling Jimmy all the way up to the heli—a nice trick, if you want to try it some time, climbing a ladder—Liz, Tom and me the second trip, to the same roof. We weren't wasting seconds; before they could get to the roof we were on—which meant figuring out which one it was, or having an observer lucky enough to spot us; we were seconds ahead however you figured it—we'd managed to get us all into one load.

It was crowded. Hell, it was a jigsaw puzzle. Five people, one of them unconscious and one of them trying to make enough space around her to drive with.

We made it. Just barely.

They had to figure us to head back to my place; but there was no other place to go. And I had a heli porthole in my roof—locked, but Liz had told Raythorne to unlock it before she'd left; she thought of everything.

Hell of a gal.

We got to my place, and we didn't land. Not right away.

First Liz took the heli down almost to ground level—I mean, within inches.

Seems we were under siege. Raythorne was firing from my front windows, and a small group was firing back. Another group was on its way to the back of the house.

I think they were planning to set it on fire.

Liz banked the heli toward the back-door group, heading right for them.

It is not a good idea to be that close to a heli rotor. Six people went flat—with a fair possibility of internal damage, broken bones, and what-have-you.

She rose over the house and headed for the front. She didn't really have to.

The people at the front of the house were flat, too. They rose very, very slowly—it's a shock to be knocked flat by a rotor wind, even if you only get it by telepathy—and Liz just hovered over them, waiting for them to make a move.

The one they made was away from the house.

After that, we landed.

Damn it, I told myself, somebody was sure as Hell going to pay for repairs. Half the windows were shot in, and there were holes and broken bits of this and that all over the living room.

Raythorne had been lying flat on the carpet, near the front window. She got up slowly when we came in and put her rifle down on the rug.

That had been a good rug, once.

Well, call it the fortunes of war. We all got down and spread Jimmy out on the rug and Raythorne started to look him over, and I headed for the phones.

Now we had a hookup, that was my first job. The telepaths were one being, and anybody knew what anybody else knew.

That was a disadvantage now and then, but it made for a single, well-directed combat unit. My phone hookup was going to help us plain ordinary human beings rig ourselves into the same sort of thing.

My second job, I was thinking as I picked up the phone, was to make my house one Hell of a lot more defensible. I'd thought of locks, and I'd thought of some other small matters.

But I hadn't set myself up against total invasion.

What the Hell, wasn't this Cub IV? The planet without a problem?

One more survivor's rule: any first-generation settlement is an armed camp—no matter what you think or what you see. Cub IV had taken twenty years to come to a head. The next world might take five seconds—and it might take another twenty years. Or thirty.

Past that, when real mapping and exploring-in-detail has begun, maybe you can relax a little. But not before that.

Explorer's rule number . . . I-forget-what. It was enough that I was still making them.

It was enough that I was still alive.

XIV

Item: the Leones weren't there any more.

A few smart boys and girls had come up with a home-made bomb. The Leone house was now a medium-sized hole in the ground.

"A few smart boys and girls"—the few who happened to get to work on it. When a telepathic network gets an idea, all of it gets the same idea. Those few just happened to be close enough to the supplies needed, so they were the ones who put the bomb together and erased the house and occupants.

Could have been anybody—anybody who'd been taken over.

And it could have been a lot more houses—except that it took time to make bombs; and except that there were comparatively few families like the Leones. Not one of them had been taken over.

That was true for very, very few families of any size.

Two- and three-person families, sure. They might go all one way, or all the other. But a first-generation colony tends to large families. When I thought about it, I realized that the group I'd collected was odd in more ways than one: of us all, only Jimmy had family ties on the planet. Raythorne's husband had died—congestive heart disease—eight years before, and they'd been a sterile couple. Liz was single, and likely to stay that way; a good many men admire competence who wouldn't have the sense, if that's what it is, to marry it. Tom's wife had died in one of those stupid accidents you hear about barely six months after they'd settled, a first baby on the way—somehow managed to switch on the ground-effects car by remote while she was in the garage. That look on Tom's face had been there before; but before there'd been nobody to hate.

And me, I'm single. Always have been. Always likely to be.

Don't ask me why, because I don't know. What I do know is that it makes a very sour joke out of that line on the application form.

A man without a family—a man without children —is the only man who is certain *not* to survive, in one very important sense. (And if I had children, I'd have a family. State-board upbringings don't seem too helpful, if you judge by results. The survival mechanism for any given adult is that adult; the survival mechanism for any given child is a family.)

Maybe some day I would find me a gal—somebody like Liz, say—and settle down. Raise a family. Help my genes survive.

Maybe. But I doubted it then and I doubt it now Nobody's perfect.

Every way but that one, I'm a survivor. And I like to work alone; in fact, the team I'd got together was beginning to get to me. I'd needed every one of them to set up the phone lines; some I was going to need again, and I knew it; maybe all of them. Raythorne's medical experience, Harry's electronics and molar-mechanics gifts, Tom and Jimmy for speed and strength (if Jimmy were going to be okay, and ready to move around, any time soon!), and Liz for plain sanity.

I wanted to be on my own. Unfortunately, I was fighting an army.

And you don't fight on army single-handed. Anyhow, not all the time.

So I picked up a lot of news. And I began to see the vague shape of the way things were going to go.

Families were split, half human and half alien. The whole world was split down the middle—on some principle I didn't understand.

The good news was that the aliens didn't understand it either. And hadn't expected it.

They'd kept saying that they couldn't be resisted.

And that had either been lack of experience talking—they'd never met minds they couldn't take over, before we came along—or the one thing a telepath can take a lifetime learning to do: plain lying.

Whatever that principle was, it would pay me to know it—it would pay all Cub IV. Suppose all future colonists were to be selected out for that factor?

And the bad news was that I did know it. I just couldn't find it.

It was in my head somewhere. The surprise at seeing two doctors and one patient as aliens—the realization that the hospital's staff would remain mostly human —fifty small things, and I couldn't put them together. The back of my head, like everybody's, *is* a good deal smarter than the front of my head. Maybe it gets that way by staying out of things—but there are times when I could cheerfully wring its neck, if the metaphor makes sense.

Why wouldn't it tell me what it knew?

I'd issued instructions over the phones—basic rules. The first one was obvious enough: Immobilize, do not kill, wherever possible.

We didn't know whether the takeovers could be turned back into human beings again. If the aliens did, they weren't saying.

The most important thing I said over the phones, aside from that, was something I wasn't entirely, absolutely sure of.

"If the person you're looking at hasn't been taken over by the aliens, then he can't be, and he won't be. If he's still human, he's safe."

It made sense—certainly the first big grab would have been for every available mind, and they'd had one full day to get their work done—and I couldn't see them trying it any other way. All the same, it wasn't knowledge, it was deduction. And deduction about an alien race can be an extraordinarily tricky thing.

I remembered one small case in point: the perfectly logical, and very humanoid, natives of Allix, to whom a hand encumbered with any sort of weapon was a sign of peace, and an empty hand a threat of force. For a race that had spent two hundred of its years on basically judo-like arts, and defeated its armed enemies quite thoroughly that way, it made sense.

For human beings, it made sense too—afterward, when you knew the relevant facts.

Beforehand . . . well, I told them what I had to tell them. And I kept my fingers crossed.

I was hanging up the phone when Liz came stalking in. That's the right word; she had her hands on her hips, and an expression on her face that let me know instantly, and thoroughly, why I'd never got married.

"Gerald Knave," she said. "Are you absolutely bent on conducting a world suicide?"

I sighed. "Well, no," I said. "I'd much rather conduct a victory. Suicide isn't what I've been planning for."

"If you've been planning for anything," she snapped. She was beautiful when she was angry. She was also beautiful when she was calm, and I preferred her that way.

"I've been———"

"You've been doing nothing," she said. "Wasting time with this telephone hookup—and nearly costing Jimmy his life———"

"He'll be okay?"

"He will, thanks to Raythorne." She was pacing up and down the living room. Her hands stayed on her hips. For some women, that's "in uniform": they can't properly tell a man off unless their hips are full of fist. Tie their arms to their sides and they can't talk. "But no thanks to you. You nearly got every one of us killed——"

"Me, too," I put in.

She nodded at me. "Oh, I realize that. I said suicide, didn't I?" She sniffed. "Good God, Jerry—we've had a whole day, and all we've done is this phone hookup——"

"You agreed to it," I said.

"I wasn't thinking," she said. "I—well, I wasn't. Not about possible guards, or the dangers . . . well, if I had been thinking, I'd have had a heli out there from the start, wouldn't I?"

"Probably," I admitted. "But we need the hookup. Without it, there isn't a thing——"

"Without it, there isn't a thing we can all do together," Liz said. "Without it, we can't make plans. We can't get together on a single campaign."

"Right." What could I say? It was my argument. Now I was going to find out what was wrong with it.

I didn't have much doubt about that. Liz got angry damn seldom. She got sane damn often. The odds were she was being both.

"The aliens know that as well as we do," she said. "Did it ever occur to you to wonder why they didn't blow up the Central Exchange before we ever reached it?"

"Well . . ."

"Of course it did," she said. She whirled around, having reached a corner of the living room, and started back toward me. "I can see that. But you never got an answer."

I said it again. "Well . . ."

"What's our only advantage over a telepathic network?" she asked.

That one I knew. "We're individuals," I said. "We can keep our plans secret. We can act on a thousand different plans——"

"Right," she said. "And there is no way for a telepath to know what we're doing, or what we're planning. Unless, of course, we are idiotic enough to tell them."

For once, I began to realize, she was wrong. She saw me relax, and that raised her voice a notch or two.

"Don't you realize that every time you put out a plan over the phone, you tell the telepaths what we're doing? You give away our only advantage? You give them every secret we've got?"

I smiled at her. I really did. "Sure," I said. For a second I thought she'd self-destruct. "But you don't call that a disadvantage, do you?"

XV

Tom Pedon pushed his way in then and saw me sitting by the phone. I don't think he saw Liz at all, which takes some doing.

"Phone's free," he said. "Good."

The thing could still be used for individual calls, as Harry had explained to me; a coded number had to be dialled to put everybody into the circuit. Tom went around by chair and picked up the phone and dialled a number.

I didn't have to ask whose.

He waited. There still wasn't any answer.

"Maybe he went to somebody else's place," I said. "Thought he'd be safer there."

"He wouldn't," Tom said. His face wasn't any worse than it had been. It wasn't any better either. "What are you two doing?"

"Arguing," I said, before Liz could get in a word.

"The Hell with all that," he said. "The Hell with everything. He didn't make it."

"Maybe—" I began.

"Maybe," Tom said. "They couldn't take him over—any more than they could take me, damn it—so they killed him. Just like the others. Tobor . . ."

He was staring at nothing.

Liz walked over to him. You wouldn't have believed it was the same voice, let alone the same woman. "We've got work to do," she said. "We're going to have to help Jimmy."

He didn't move. "The Hell with Jimmy."

She put a hand on his arm. "Tom—"

That didn't move him either. "The Hell with everything," he said. "They got him, that's all. They couldn't take him over, so they got him."

"They'll get Jimmy, too," she said, "unless we help."

Very slowly, he nodded. "Right," he said. "They beamed the kid."

"And he won't make it unless we help out," Liz said. "Raythorne can't do it all alone. Jimmy needs you."

Tom nodded. "I guess," he said.

(Liz told me, some while later: "Love will activate some people, and hate will activate some. Need will activate most, I think—and the ones it won't work on may not be worth talking to." Sometimes I wonder if she'd reached the answer before I did.)

They went out and left me. All right, Knave: you're alone. Now do your stuff.

I picked up the situation and it looked like stalemate. The aliens had taken over a lot of us—something less than half, by what I was getting, but not a great deal less—and killed some more. But human beings were fighting back, and the telepaths had had losses—a few dead, most incapacitated one way or another: tied up like Laia Kodorko and Miles Haddison (they'd been removed out of the streets to nice comfortable quarters in the Government Building nearby. They'd acted totally unconscious throughout—which was true of every telepath we immobilized, once he'd tested his bonds and found he couldn't get out), wounded like several under guard and surrounded by tubing at the hospital, locked in and guarded by a few people who turned out to be minorities in their own families, and hadn't got the jump on the human remnant.

The telepaths couldn't wipe us out—I knew that, and we'd just had an interesting time proving it—and they couldn't drive us off the planet.

The question was, what could we do about them?

Kill every alien we see? Kill every one we can find? Sure.

And then what? Suppose it turns out, later, that your dead alien could have turned right back into Aunt Minnie?

I shook my head; I was getting fuzzy. The taken-over humans weren't alien. But there were aliens, living on Cub IV—somewhere.

If we found those—Aunt Minnie wouldn't be in the picture.

We'd kill—if we had to. As a last resort. If every other method of persuasion failed.

If—well, do you really want to wipe out an intelligent race? Never mind that they hit you first.

We won't be dictated to—no. But maybe we've grown up a little. We don't like genocide very much, not any more. Not even on aliens.

So, if we found out where they were, we wouldn't just hand-make a few bombs and drop them. No. Instead . . .

There were all sorts of fascinating possibilities. I sat down and thought about a few of them. Maybe stalemate wasn't the word. Maybe, just maybe, there was a victory we could pull out of this situation.

Hope, somebody had said, springs eternal in the human breast. And there was an older legend—that hope had come to give aid to humanity, out of Pandora's Box.

Of course, everything else had to come out first.

The "everything else" we were trying to deal with.

I picked up the phone.

I didn't call everybody: no need for it, not then.

Instead, I called a number I knew was going to be answered by somebody who'd been taken over.

This conversation wasn't for human ears, unless you count my pair. Human ears, in fact, wouldn't have gone for it at all.

Essentially, what I said was: "Take me to your leader."

That went through several convolutions of explaining, and even more spirals and curves of persuasion. The aliens—the real aliens, not our human imitations—were understandably reluctant to let any immune human being know where they were, or even what they looked like.

I was sweating when I put down the phone. I'd been waiting, every instant, for somebody to come back into the living room—Tom or Liz or Raythorne or even a taped-up, strapped-together Jimmy. (Harry didn't bother me. Harry could be explained to, I was sure; and the likeliest thing was that he'd just accept the conversation as mournfully as he accepted everything else, and go on about his own doings, whatever they were now the phone linkage was complete.)

The famous Knave luck was running strong. Nobody came in. I had my privacy.

And my persuasive powers were in fairly good order too. For instance:

"I could have killed the human beings in your network over and over. I could have killed them one by one—I had the opportunities, from Laia Kodorko and Miles Haddison to the hospital and on to the Central Exchange. I stunned where I could, and wounded where I had to. You can take that as evidence that I don't like killing. I'm not out to exterminate you."

"Then what is your objective?" that dead voice asked me. It could have been a man or a woman. It doesn't matter. Nothing mattered about that voice except that it wasn't human any more. "You cannot be preparing to leave our world."

"Of course not," I said. "I don't leave. And humans don't leave. And won't have to."

"Then there is no objective."

"We might be able to help you," I said.

"We have no need——"

"You thought you had no need," I said. "But you never ran into people you couldn't control, either, did you? There might be more like us—things that aren't you, and aren't human either, and can't be controlled. And if they discover you, they might decide to exterminate you—entirely. No way to judge the motives of an alien race. But it's not wise to assume them to be good for you."

There was a slight pause. Consideration? Consultation? "Agreed," the voice said. "It is not wise to assume your motives to be good for us; quite as you say."

"I didn't say they were. I said they didn't involve exterminating you—and I said that the human race, which does not want to exterminate you—not yet —might be able to give you some help. We just might have some things to talk over."

"What sort of things?" the voice said.

"An arrangement," I said. "An agreement. A treaty of peace. Any kind of a thing like that."

"An agreement—with you?" For a second there was almost a tone in the voice; but it wasn't a pleasant tone.

"We can discuss it."

"Then discuss with one of us," the voice said. "One of your race who has joined the network."

"No can do," I said. "One of us would be shot by somebody, no matter where we were. Too dangerous. But I figure that you—the inhabitants, you know who I mean—live out of the danger zone. You'd have to: away from the city, away from any human habitation. Or we'd have turned you up long ago. Out there, where there's nobody to shoot at us, we'd be safe enough to concentrate on discussion."

Another pause. "You are very plausible," the voice said. "But we have no need of talk with you."

"I think you do," I said. "You're bright." Well, they had to be, didn't they? And (I was assuming —rightly, as it turned out, but how could it have been any other way?) they'd have all the knowledge and experience of the human beings they'd taken over to tap. One million times zero is still zero, but there had been some bright people in that batch. Right on back to number one, Johnny James—one Hell of a bright kid, he'd been.

"And?"

"I've run the situation through," I said. "The best I come up with, for you, is stalemate. A constant war —never winning, never losing."

"We are familiar with the term."

From human brains, like the rest of the language. "I'm assuming you're bright, too—and you'll come up with the same answer if you run it through. Understand me: that's the *best* I come up with for you. We've been holding back."

"We do not believe that."

"Because none of the humans you took over know it," I said. "Okay, none of them are supposed to know it. But I've got a ready relay to the Comity through space-four—no colonist is supposed to have that, but I'm a little special. You'll have found out about that."

A reputation is a useful thing, once in a while. It may even help get you out of the messes it gets you into. "And what will your relay accomplish?"

I sounded very plausible. "There are weapons these colonists don't know about. There are fighting techniques they've never heard of. And in the normal course of events they'd never need them. But I've got my relay—which means that I have them on call."

That was the longest silence yet. They knew humans told lies. They'd said as much, a few seconds before. But they couldn't really have believed it; a lie is something contrary to the entire life experience of a telepath.

They'd be warning themselves that I might be handing them a line. But they couldn't be sure . . .

In the end, they had to believe me.

"Leave by the front door of your house," the voice said. "You will be met and conveyed."

"How?"

"You will be met and conveyed." Click. End message.

Well, all right; I really didn't need any more. The rest, as they say, was obvious.

XVI

So I opened the front door and went out into the peaceful early evening.

Sure.

First of all, I went looking for Liz. They'd turned my bedroom—my beautiful bedroom!—into a hospital extension, and Jimmy was in the middle of it, on a semiforce-semisolid support bed, under a canopy that was nothing short of magnificent, either in effect or in price. He was swaddled more or less like a mummy. Raythorne had rigged tubing from somewhere, and a fractionator. The thing had to be a fractionator, hooked into the blood-supply line; apparently she'd built it herself, or called in Harry for help. I recognized pieces of a 3V of mine, and parts of two very fine, absolutely irreplaceable speakers.

One end of the tubing was running into Jimmy. The other end was attached to Tom.

Well, I spent a second thanking God for the fractionator. It had been a fairly recent invention, even on Earth—but depend on Raythorne to keep up with the novelties, the ones that paid off.

Without it, we'd have needed to find somebody with Jimmy's particular blood type, and God alone knew what that might be. With it, anybody would do who had human blood to begin with; the fractionator realigned the blood molecules, or something—it has to do with

99

enzymes, is all I recall—and let Type A blood go right on in (its special, deadly qualities filtered out or changed) as Type B, or whatever.

Harry was sleeping in a scrollwork chair. Liz was standing over Tom—oh, Tom was laid out on a real-silk couch!—and Raythorne was fiddling with some detail of the tubing or the bandaging.

She didn't look up. Liz did. "The beam got him in the side, below the ribs," she said. "Made its own cautery—at that he's lucky to be alive."

A slug in that particular spot wouldn't have done too much harm, if it had gone wide of vital organs nearby. But a beam tends to spread when it hits—a tendency most beam guns foster—and that meant Jimmy was missing quite a chunk.

"He is going to make it?"

"She says so." Liz nodded over at Raythorne. She finished with whatever it was she was doing and looked up.

"He'll be all right, Jerry," she said. "I was wondering when you'd come to ask."

"When I had time," I said. "And I don't have any now. I'm on my way out."

Tom began to sit up; Liz pushed him back down. "Out?" he croaked.

"Out?" Liz said. "Why?"

"Necessary," I said. And left it at that. "If I'm not back in—ten hours, forget me. You're in control, Liz: do whatever you have to do."

Tom and Raythorne, at the same moment, said: "But——"

"But nothing," I said. "I've got to go. And I'm

coming back. But I plan for all contingencies—even the most unlikely ones.''

''I'll come with you,'' Tom said. It was a Hell of a statement from a man lying down with a tube in his arm, talking in a weak croak.

''You're needed here,'' I said. ''And this is a solo job.''

Harry never woke up.

Then I took precautions.

Every one I could think of. Personal armor, a thorough set of weapons—including two actual grenades, so valuable I'd rather have to stomp an enemy position to death, if it came to that—my portable phone keyed to my private number (and now, thanks to Harry, keyed to the whole Exchange).

Two reasons:

First, I might be shot by a human being. The presumption had to be that anybody walking around loose was an alien; human beings were staying under cover. Anybody who recognized me would hold his fire (I hoped)—but lots of the colonists had never seen me, knew me only by reputation, and maybe second-hand reputation at that. And a lot of people wouldn't wait for recognition; they'd shoot as soon as they saw any figure loose, just near enough to be identified as human.

Come to think of it, maybe even further than that. They knew as well as I did there were aliens out there.

And second, I wasn't absolutely wedded to my basic theory. As far as I could see, a telepath couldn't lie—he'd have no practice, no experience; the whole concept would be totally foreign to him.

What the Hell, I've been wrong before.

"Walk out your front door." It was a fine invitation. But I couldn't be entirely sure what I was being invited to.

So I wore my formals.

Every steel, beryllium, vanadium, aluminum and force-field inch of them.

I didn't look very much like a human being—in that getup, whether it's for armor or for an atmosphere suit, nobody does. I looked like something better.

I looked like staying alive.

And, looking like staying alive, I marched out my front door.

Nobody shot at me.

In fact, for an entire minute—which is a much longer time than you think it is; my God, that minute seemed like thirty or forty years—nothing whatever happened; I was suspended, armored, ready—and waiting.

Especially waiting.

Then the wind hit me, and I knew.

XVII

It was a heli, of course. One man driving the thing, a stranger to me—but I was no stranger to him. He banked over my head and set down a hundred feet away, in a large clear intersection.

I walked over to him, not in any hurry.

"We will go to the place," he said in that dead voice. He made a gesture toward my seat in the heli.

Nothing to lose: I got in, and we were off.

Call it two hours. I could locate the spot, but there's no good reason to any more; they'll have moved it. The first checks had missed because these particular aliens were neither land nor water types: they were swamp beings. They looked like clams, clams maybe four feet across, with transparent greenish shells. I couldn't have seen all of them there were—not even all in that particular settlement. I did see better than twenty at one time or another, allowing for confusion as one dropped under the swamp surface and another rose.

The place bubbled all the time I was there—slowly and loudly. And it stank.

My pilot didn't seem to mind. Maybe the aliens didn't have a sense of smell.

It was somewhere during that conversation, by the way, that I gave them a name. After a while, I found, I had to call them something—and Vesci sounded good enough. Traditional Latin name for a new genus, and it's connected with the Latin word for "eaters" or "devourers".

They were as happy to be referred to as Vesci as when I called them aliens. And no happier, and no less; names didn't matter.

How could they, to a telepathic race?

We got down to business fairly fast. They weren't really willing to agree that a stalemate was the best they could get out of us, but they wanted to know what I had to offer.

I said: "Technology. Ways of doing things."

"We need nothing," the pilot said. He served as translator; I'm not a mind-reader, and the Vesci—from now on, I'll keep them christened—couldn't get into my head.

"Travel," I said.

"We need no new ways to travel. Animals of our world take us where we wish. Now human beings will also take us."

Sure: they could ride piggy-back on anything they could control.

And the human beings they controlled had access to technology, too; even if I managed to sell the Vesci the idea, what goods did I have for trade?

Well . . .

"There is much we can teach you," I said. "There is much knowledge that we have, which you lack." There had to be—or the Vesci would have been refusing to leave the Comity worlds, instead of the reverse.

"The minds we have added contain much knowledge."

"There's more. And—suppose we took those minds away?"

"You cannot do so." The dead voice sounded just a trifle less certain.

I raised my eyebrows at the damn clams. A particularly large bubble rose, and popped, and stank. "Suppose we were to take them off the planet," I said. "Leave here the people you can't control—and take away the ones you can. Either take them, or kill them—one way or the other, they're lost to you."

I hoped I was right: but there had to be some sort of distance limit to telepathy. If there weren't, then why hadn't the Vesci taken over the universe several thousand years before?

"Their knowledge remains." But the voice sounded even shakier.

"It takes time to get it, and to assort it," I said. "And there is more. And—without your human help, how long do you think you'd last against a concerted assault?"

"We cannot be resisted," the pilot said.

I gave him a friendly grin. "Sure you can," I told him. "I'm doing it. Lots of us—more than half—are doing it. And we'll go right on doing it."

"What do you offer?" he said after a second.

"Knowledge, and peace," I said.

"You will not take away the human beings we speak of?"

"Not if we can come to an agreement here and now," I said. Even then I knew I was lying. Maybe the pilot would have known. But habits are tough to break: ten to one the Vesci believed me.

"You are the leader of the humans who resist us," the pilot said.

"Without me, they'd go on just the same," I said. "Wipe me out and somebody would come along to take my place." That was maybe half a lie: I had, as I'd discovered, a reputation. It was easy for me to stand up and provide a focal point.

Somebody else could do it—would do it if I were erased from the picture. Liz, on a bet. But even Liz, with all her sanity and strength, wouldn't be the same . . .

And it'd take time—valuable time . . .

"This is not fact," the pilot said. "This is your opinion."

"My educated, experienced opinion," I said. It was all the weight I had to put on it.

It wasn't enough. The damn fool drew a gun and shot me.

It was a clean hit. Couldn't have been anything else, at the range. My armor soaked up the beam like sunlight, with about as much effect—the great disadvantage of beam weapons is that they have no shocking power; if you can soak up the beam energy, there's nothing left to knock you down with. A solid slug, even if it bounces off armor, leaves the receiver flat on his back.

He showed no surprise. He fired again.

That time, I wasn't there when the beam arrived. Instead, I was heading over into the depths of the swamp—straight into the worst of the damn smell, too—toward a green transparent clam.

I had my own gun out—holding it butt-foremost. I had no idea what would kill one of the Vesci, but a tap with the butt seemed less likely to be fatal than a slug from the barrel.

And I didn't want to be fatal.

I seldom do. It buys little, and it costs like Hell.

I only wanted to demonstrate that I could be fatal any time I chose—and that the decision was theirs.

The pilot whirled. He wasn't going to give me that beam a third time: he'd learned his lesson, and if he did manage to miss he was odds on to hit a clam.

But my face didn't look armored. (Looks are often deceptive.) And he must have fancied himself a fair pitcher—or the Vesci did, from his mind or that of someone who knew him.

He threw the beamer.

Good shot, too—and leading me just enough so that it would have hit me square on the bridge of my nose if I'd kept on going in a straight line at established speed.

But (as they say) no. I saw the throw as he turned —he was fast, barely took time to aim—and stopped dead and ducked.

The thing went whistling on by. I hoped the green shells were tougher than they looked.

It didn't hit one; it hit the swamp, gave up a splash of tiny, smelly drops of whatever in Hell that swamp was made of, and sank out of sight without a sound.

By the time it was gone I had my arms around a clam.

It quivered and tried to shut; I held it open.

A couple of seconds went by. The pilot said: "What do you mean to do?" in the same perfectly calm voice.

"Kill one of you, damn it," I said, "if you don't stop trying to kill me."

Stalemate. (Those green shells were tough—maybe a slug would have got through and hit a vital spot, or something, and maybe not.) While I was trying to kill one of the Vesci, the pilot would be trying to kill me—with another beamer, maybe, or whatever else he had going for him. And the rest of the clams would be helping, if they could. Aided by other animals from the vicinity . . .

Maybe I could get one by the time they got me. Maybe I could get two.

But I thought I knew how they would see things. After all, they were telepaths.

"We will return you safely to your place," the pilot said. His arms were at his sides. "Let go of us."

Death is not a pleasant experience.

And for a telepath, it must be even worse—you have to live through it. When one of the Vesci dies, or when one of the humans in that network dies—every one of the Vesci, every person in that network, feels the death.

I didn't think they would give up one of them for one of me.

Not quite that baldly. For a telepathic race, every death of any member feels like suicide—a suicide you remember next day when you wake up again.

I let go. Cautiously and slowly. I started to pick my way out of the swamp.

The pilot watched me for a few seconds. Then he went back to the heli, parked conveniently on a patch of dry land.

He was sitting in the first seat when I got there.

"No," I said. "Once we're out of immediate physical touch, I would much rather be piloting."

The pilot sighed. It was the most human sound I had heard from him. He got out of his seat and into the passenger's bucket.

I climbed in and grabbed the stick.

He didn't try to kill me more than three times on the way home. Hell, I figure that shows great forbearance.

A heli is fairly stable; if he'd got me, he might have survived. It was no longer one-for-one; the bargain no longer applied. I'd figured on five tries at least.

Well, maybe he was just slow. New at the killing trade, say. But he only got three tries in. None of them are worth talking about.

Do I have to add that none of them succeeded?

XVIII

Somehow, I don't think I was very convincing, there in the swamp.

If the Vesci had really believed that stalemate was their best chance—and that there was a distinct chance of pulling all the Vesci-ridden humans off the planet right away—they might have done one of two things.

They might have proceeded cautiously—trying to better their position, but doing it a little at a time.

And they might have tried for one grand blowup —getting all the human beings available at once, and giving them an unbeatable edge.

Instead, the war went on.

I did get home, and was let in by Liz, who looked somber. The look was due to lack of sleep: she'd spent more actual waking time with Jimmy than Raythorne had—and I ordered her off to bed; she went without a murmur.

Nobody shot at me. Nobody even tried to throw anything at me.

And I stayed safe for quite a while, considering.

I used the phone link to pass on the details of my talk with the Vesci, and such details about the Vesci as I had—advising people not to go out to the swamps except in force and with real armor, since they were certain to be opposed both by Vesci-owned humans and by any available local animals.

And it made for a minor score against Liz's complaint with the link system: I did tell people something they had to know—the terms of the war they were in, and just what the enemy was like, as far as I'd been able to get it—and if I told the Vesci as well, what harm did it do? The Vesci already knew it.

I stayed inside, and I kept thinking.

Somewhere in the back of my head, I knew what the difference was between a person the Vesci could take over, and one they couldn't.

I got no nearer to it.

And—all right, how had they known where I was going to be, and when, by the Exchange building, when they'd started the shooting? Tom's explanation did hold water, but it didn't sound right.

I think I knew the answer to that one, too. But I didn't want to know it.

So I was convinced that I didn't.

And I kept thinking, too, about the threat I'd tossed the Vesci: take their human network away from them. Could it actually be done?

Space-four is expensive, and the job would be risky. (How many ship commanders would you lose to the Vesci? And what would the Vesci do in command of a starship?) I do swing a little weight—but not enough to snap out my communicator and bark an order and get me sixty ships with alternate captains on every ship.

I didn't really think I could get them off the planet.

Hell, I didn't really think I'd want to try, even if I had the authority. Pile on all the alternate captains you like, at some point there is going to be a Vesci-owned human being in charge of a ship over Cub IV . . . and the Vesci have no objection to killing at all, so long as it doesn't take place inside their minds.

(Another aspect of telepathy, maybe: can a telepath have any empathy with nontelepathic creatures, no matter how intelligent? I swear I asked myself that question then—sitting in my house, wondering what to do—and never saw the answer embedded in it.)

But maybe they could be segregated . . .

Maybe, just maybe, I could take on a few of the humans that weren't human any more, and stack them away permanently where they couldn't do any harm.

It had happened to most of the Vesci-humans at the hospital. It had happened to Laia Kodorko and Miles Haddison.

Maybe, I told myself, I could make it happen to some more.

A day or so had gone by. People kept calling and there was damned little to tell them. I had a shot in reserve, but it had to stay in reserve just then.

I ate and slept. We kept guard schedules, but there wasn't much disturbance; my place had earned some respect, and it got some.

Jimmy was improving little by little, but he wasn't conscious. He had all the blood he needed, but Tom was still a handy orderly, and he was used as much as possible—Liz's notion, Raythorne's approval. He didn't sink back into that darkness of his again.

Harry spent a lot of time working. My place had a fair amount of loose wiring and tools, and he'd got some more. I asked him what he was working on and he stared at me. Wasn't it obvious?

Well, no.

"Telepathy has to take place in terms of some sort of detectable force, doesn't it?" he said.

"I have no idea," I said.

"Well, it does." He was explaining matters to a small child again. "It affects human minds, and a human mind is an electromagnetic system, basically."

I nodded, to show him that I was keeping up.

He nodded back. "Whatever affects an electromagnetic system has to be an electromagnetic effect," he said. "I want to try and find it. If I can locate it—get it in terms of a tuning frequency. . . ."

I could see the advantages. And some disadvantages, too. And I wasn't at all sure of his premise. If I drop a large rock on my radio and smash it to unusable bits, I'm affecting an electromagnetic system. Is the rock an electromagnetic effect?

But I didn't argue him out of it. For one thing, he was so busy he was very nearly cheerful.

For another, it was occupational therapy; he was safer in my place than he would have been anywhere else, and on tap if I did need him, and in the meantime he'd found himself something to do.

Having nothing to do has ruined kings and great empires.

I didn't say that, by the way. I wish I had, but the credit goes to an Ancient Roman poet, name of Catullus.

That was the state I was in, thinking of Roman poets, for God's sake, while I was putting on my armor. I chased the thing out of my head and went back to lists of colonists. Between them, Liz and Raythorne and Tom knew everybody, or just about; and I could check my own memory of phone calls, link-phone calls and replies, and such to tell me which were still dependably human and which had turned into something else.

I had a nice long list of Something Elses.

I was winnowing it down by location, home setup, neighbors, everything I could think of. This was a first foray, and it had to be good. I could take on the tougher jobs when the easier ones were cleaned up—when I had less working against me.

I thought about Tobor Raisford.

He still wasn't answering his phone. Nobody had seen him.

The probability was that Tom was right. And Tobor was single: he'd come out, single, fifteen years before.

Tobor's house might have only one person in it.

Then again, the person would be Tobor . . .

I finally settled on Rame Janssen. He had a farm, lived alone (wife and two children dead in a landslide the year before—they'd all gone out exploring, and Rame had come back), and had responded over the phone in the voice I'd come to recognize.

He looked easy; as I remembered him, he wasn't even a very big sort of guy.

By then I had my armor on.

Well, off we go to work for the day. Daddy said goodbye to all (excepting the unconscious Jimmy), and shook hands all round, and set out for the office.

In full armor, and driving my own car.

The car was a little special, too. I had everything going for me, including spare slugs and spare guns in a dash compartment.

It did look awfully easy, when the door shut behind me. A cinch, I thought.

That thought may win me the Overconfidence Trophy for the decade.

XIX

I got out of the car. That was my first mistake.

(Well, when I come to think about it, maybe my first mistake had been landing on Cub IV. But why bother with such regrets?)

I had parked about a hundred feet from the house, a long low single-story job that looked like an Old Earth Farmland reproduction. The road curved deeply out to my left as I came to the place, and I'd stopped on the curve as it began to return toward the front door: the whole house was a hundred feet ahead and slightly to my right, with a big picture window and a stretch of slat wall before the door, away over at the other side of the front. It seemed a Hell of an inconvenient way to lay a driveway, but maybe the Janssens had thought it was picturesque, or traditional.

Or something. What it was, just then, was damn near deadly.

I was in flat land: next to no cover whatever, all the way to the house. A bunch of bushes standing in an ornamental sort of way maybe fifty feet to my right, straight across; and no other cover anywhere in sight. Nice flat farmland.

The first shot didn't do me any harm: my armor soaked it up without a blink. It had been fired from the house itself—right through the picture window, which, I noticed, no longer had any glass in it.

A fight? Or was Rame just clearing the decks for action? Rame—I meant the thing that had taken him over.

If he had a hand beamer and kept on using it, I was home free. But you don't take that sort of chance; I went to my right, in a crouch and moving fast.

The second shot knocked me onto my back.

Somebody with a slug gun had hit me in the left shoulder. The armor bounced the slug off, but transmitted the momentum, which was considerable.

I'd been watching the window. No flash.

Rame had company.

I lit rolling, and went for the ornamental bush. I had my own slug gun in my right hand, but I hadn't had a decent chance to use it. I got nicely behind the bush and shifted to a position I could fire from. Then I did a stupid thing: I fired into that window.

I didn't figure to hit anybody—whoever had been using the beamer was standing well back and out of sight. But shooting back always helps; it shakes them up a little.

Gives you a chance for a second shot that *will* be a good one.

I realized that the shot located me, but that didn't seem to matter. Where the Hell else could I have been?

One man with a beamer inside the house. One with a slug gun—and where was he? Someplace ahead of me. I hadn't seen a flash. For the moment I was pinned down, considering things.

The guy with the beamer was no problem: my armor was good for that. The one with the slug gun—

The one with the slug gun fired again. A slug has a

nasty whining sound when it passes right over your head.

I had him: he was over to my left, and he had to be round the side of the house, just leaning forward to sight and shoot. Anywhere else, he'd have been in plain sight.

So I snapped a shot that way, trying to chip the corner of the house. Give him something to think about.

Somewhere in there I realized my mistake.

The damn bush was on fire.

A beamer is a silent weapon—whether you call that an advantage or not depends on what you do with it. The mind behind this one had been smart. It couldn't hurt me, at least not on one very good shot; maybe it could toast me.

My armor would stand up to heat, of course—what else is a beam?—but the more it was forced to deal with the bush, the less energy it would have left over to maintain a field against anything else. A good, well-aimed slug, say.

I wasn't fighting two people.

I was fighting one person—with two bodies.

They had to figure to drive me away from the bush toward my right—over toward the front door. The man inside would be ready and waiting. The guy around the corner of the house would have a nice clear shot too.

Going to my left was heading straight into the slug gun, with my armor taking its time, maybe a full second, about readjusting after the fire.

Going back was a little safer—the bush, burning or not, was a slight screen. But there wasn't anything back there.

If I fell back twenty yards, what did I do next? Set up light housekeeping?

I hoped the Vesci were figuring me for a smart move. Back or to either side, I would be doing the intelligent thing, by the book—and losing, too.

So I went through the bush, standing.

Even inside the armor I felt the heat rise. For about a second I was surrounded by flames—totally surrounded, like a man being burned at the stake.

I was stone blind to everything but that fire. And stone deaf, too: all I could hear was the crackle and hiss of the bush going up.

I thumbed a belt button and a polarizing square went into action in front of my face—part of the armor, rigged to work that way.

My eyes adjust fast. The guy with the slug gun had fired again during that second—and a bullet doesn't sound any pleasanter when it's going by a few feet in front of your nose.

He'd led me, of course, figured me to keep moving—not to stay in the fire, for God's sake! What kind of sense did that make?

I heard the whine through the crackle-and-hiss that was my temporary universe. I began to be able to see.

I looked for the picture window. Nobody visible.

The bush went right on flaming. I went into a crouch. Maybe my armor would take a slug or a beam on top of the fire; maybe not. I watched the window.

Another second. Nobody fired. Maybe I was a shock to them: who walks straight *into* a flaming holocaust, for God's sake? There was a figure at the right of the window, a silhouette, appearing, diving back and then appearing again.

I gave it a slug. Clean miss, damn it. I got a beam back by way of mutual trade, but I didn't have to test the armor against it. It went wide to my left.

The fire was dying down. I didn't think about where I was going. I started for the front door in the same crouch—not a straight line. Skirmish zigzagging.

Nobody on Cub IV had seen much of that. Maybe the Vesci had never seen it at all, any time.

I was firing as I went—not with the slug gun.

My left hand held a beamer. I began toasting the house. It wasn't a target I could miss—talk about hitting the side of a barn—and everywhere the beam lit a few flames sprang up.

I'd taken a guess and been right: that fancy-Dan house was just too traditional to be built out of the non-inflammable plastic imitation most of us used. The Janssens had used real wood—Cub IV had trees, it was always possible.

Most people didn't bother. But the people who'd built that house—

I started as much as I could over by the far corner, where the slug gun had to be sitting. He fired back at me once, but I was on a zig and he fired into a zag—easy to do if you're not used to the maneuver.

Flat against the front door, I felt a little heat begin to come toward me from the house. My screen was still up, and I could see fine. I saw him when he came out from behind his burning corner.

Rame Janssen. He came out very fast and very low—the smart way. I'd been aiming for his body—I didn't have time to pick my spots any better, had to go for the biggest target—and blew the top of his head off.

Shock reaction. I had the time to use it against the beamer in the house, and any others; they'd all died with Rame.

I wasted almost all of it. I'd died with him too.

The war had been going on—actively—for three days or better. Rame was the first person I'd killed.

And I hadn't expected to . . .

I came out of it faster than they did. I was into the house—parts of the front were burning merrily, but the fire would take a while to spread, it was a roomy place—and had the beamer in my sights before he'd turned around to face me.

Pardon the pronoun. And for the Vesci, I suppose I ought to say *it*. But this one was female human, whoever was using her mind for the moment.

A big woman in her thirties, orange hair and muscles on her muscles. I'd seen her around—she was tough to miss—but couldn't recall the name. She swung toward me, saw me holding the gun and relaxed.

I said: "What happened to the peace treaty?"

"You did not expect us to remain peaceful after you were gone," she said. The dead voice was the same.

"I didn't expect—" No, it wasn't.

It was a human voice trying to imitate the flat sound of those others.

She hadn't noticed my pause. "—expect anybody like you," I said. "What are you doing here?" I wanted to hear the voice again.

The fire pushed us back a few feet. It was hard to hear her over the roar. In a little while the damn building was going to come down; well, before then we'd be out.

"I was driven from another place," she said. Still doing the imitation. "I came here to acquire food and equipment. I knew Rame Janssen was one of us."

The Vesci hadn't talked like that. *Us . . . I . . .*

they were being used the way human beings used them. I didn't change expression any. "Rame is dead," I said.

"I know that," she said. "And now you will kill me. But we are too many. In the end——"

"Kill you, Hell," I said. "You're my secret weapon."

I was in motion. She tried to beam me as I came toward her, but the armor was soaking it up again without trouble.

I hit her in the stomach with my fist. A good solid blow; makes them easier to move around if you're in a hurry.

And I was in a hurry. The building was flaming higher. I could hear roof beams cracking.

She folded with the punch and I ducked my shoulder, put her over it and headed straight on, same direction.

The side wall didn't have a window in it at that point. Didn't need one, either; it was mostly gone. The fire was high, but it was a thin curtain; with speed, she'd make it.

I got her through fast. She was still conscious, but she hadn't had time to put up any opposition.

Outside the house I slowed down—a lot. That was one big heavy girl.

She tried a roundhouse swing with the beamer, aiming at my head. Admirable notion, but the armor bounced it off and gave her a sore hand. I rode with it, mostly.

I'd taken my hands off her. Behind me the house was burning. Behind me, too, Rame Janssen was dead . . . well, I didn't have to think about that. Not then.

She swung again, and hit armor again. A few of the colonists had working personal armor—some probably force-field stuff like mine, and equally good—but not many. And most had packed it away long ago; on Cub IV what did you need it for?

Now they'd be digging for it. But it'd take time to find, time to put on and use. And this girl didn't have any at all.

Unfair, in a way. I slugged her on the chin and took her to the car.

XX

By the time I had the car started I heard engines.

Somebody was coming overhead in a heli.

The big girl was draped unconscious in the seat next to me. I thought about tying her, then figured I'd have time to bop her if she came to inconveniently; I just strapped her in, clip-ons that take less than a second, and did the same to myself.

I started the trip back—turning around right off the marked road into the Janssen grass—well, the Janssens wouldn't be taking care of it any more—and then out along the road. The roar of the motor overhead got louder.

I shoved the pedal down. The road-dust was clouding up the side windows as the ground-effects car whipped along. My chance of outrunning a heli was zero.

But a ground-effects car is fairly good at taking fast reverse curves. I began taking them—weaving all the Hell over the road, a trail like a snake.

The dust clouds got higher and thicker.

And the heli began to back off.

Those crazy curves were creating eddies in the air around me—big ones. I was giving the heli pilot a bumpy ride; unless he was very, very good he'd want to stay well back of this flipping maniac.

He wasn't that good—or else he was just plain cautious, a trait I greatly admire. And deplore, in my enemies.

He dropped back. Maybe fifty feet behind me—just about the limit of my little eddies.

I didn't quit flipping the car around.

The pilot was firing at me.

This one used slugs. I saw one hit the rear window and bounce off—I said my car was a little special; you couldn't call it bulletproof, but it will discourage most slugs. At the speed we were going the impact made the thing waver a little, and I had to wrestle it back into pattern.

A nice, curving snake-trail—not quite predictable.

Another shot—clean miss. Hit the road ahead of me. I saw the dust fountain, and we were past it. Farmland flashed by on both sides.

It was a long way to town. Not quite so long to the place I was looking for.

I curved again. The heli's roar seemed to get louder. I looked back fast, decided it was my imagination and kept my eyes on the road. His third shot starred my rear window, a little to the right of center. The glassex didn't break, but it cracked one thousand ways from the center of impact. And the car wavered again.

It was a great time for my passenger to start to wake up. I felt her stir, took one very quick glance and used my left hand to return her to her dreams, if any.

The heli pilot was having a better idea.

He was rising—that accounted for the change in engine sound I'd heard; he was feeding power to the thing—and getting above my zone of influence. The air-eddies couldn't hurt him. On the other hand, unless he had a bomb or something to drop on me. . . .

No. He was even smarter than that. He went up, passed me and then came down again. He hovered right on the road—maybe one foot above the ground. In a modern heli, this is not a frighteningly difficult maneuver—Liz had done something of the same sort to rid my place of its attacking band, when we'd come back from the Exchange.

The difficulty was all mine.

The one thing I couldn't do was drive straight into that hurricane. A wheeled car would have been in trouble; a ground-effects car would be tossed away like a chip.

There were fields to both sides: Cub IV's version of triticale. The stuff seems to grow nearly anywhere human beings can grow; except for the Comity worlds, it's pretty well replaced wheat, rye and most other grains. Cub IV grew a lot of it—a world of peaceful farmers.

At that season (triticale got two crops a year out of Cub IV's weather) the stuff was about seven feet high.

I turned left, straight into it.

I didn't really have much choice.

The car didn't like my decision at all. It bucked and tipped and coughed—instead of a normal flat cushion for a ground-effect wind, here we were in the middle of all this tall stuff.

The heli sat right where it was. Another shot went by, but it was a long miss; I was wavering all over the place without even trying. How long I could keep it up was an interesting question. Sooner or later some of the triticale was going to get in and foul a part, or else the whole drive was going to quit in sheer disgust at what it was being asked to do . . .

Or, of course, the heli might have something to contribute . . .

My passenger stirred again. That, I told myself, was all I needed—one more little problem to wrestle with.

The car tilted about ten degrees, and returned to normal.

The heli was overhead, someplace.

I reached out to shelve my passenger . . . and didn't slug her.

Instead, I twisted her nose. Hard.

She yelped. Very nearly a human yelp—not quite, but nothing like the dead voices I was used to hearing.

Upstairs, the heli's sound didn't change. Well, it hadn't really been enough . . .

I twisted the nose again. More yelps. This time she got her hands up past the straps and tried to drag my hand off. Then she tried to beat it to death. These attempts accomplished nothing much except to add a few extra twinges to the nose I was holding.

I let it go.

The heli coughed. At the same time my car tilted a little—not more than five degrees, I think—but the heli was in the right spot and I got a nice look at it.

It was side-slipping.

As I watched, it righted itself. So did the car, thank God. I fought my way through the waves of growing grain. The big girl was trying to get at me with both hands, bent into long-nailed claws.

I batted her hands down with my free one, and reached for her nose again. This twist was an especially hard one.

The heli went round in a wide arc. It sideslipped again.

The girl said: "What are you doing?" It was a better imitation than the yelp.

"Sooner or later, the pilot is going to crash, up there," I said.

"We will not allow you——"

"Go ahead," I said. "Stop me." She was trying. She had her hands clawed again. I batted them down—hard, this time, with the edge of my palm.

She yelped.

Then I twisted her nose again.

She yelped some more.

"Sooner or later, you're going to crash, up there," I said. "You can't take sudden, severe twinges of unpredictable pain. And you're getting them broadcast right from here. You can't even cut her out of the net." That had been the only uncertainty; but it hadn't seemed likely that the Vesci would let go of anybody they'd once grabbed, under any circumstances.

It wasn't anything like certain that they *could* let go, whether or not they wanted to.

I gave the nose one last twist—a good strong one. The girl yelped.

The heli almost did crash, right then and there —which would have landed it on top of my gallant little beetle of a car. But the pilot recovered at the last second.

Then he went away.

I kept on slapping the hands down and twisting the nose, and fighting my way through amber waves of, until the heli was a speck. Maybe a minute or so.

Then I slugged the girl unconscious, and got the Hell back on the road.

XXI

Home is the sailor, home from the sea. I didn't have any trouble to speak of on the way back: the heli was gone for good, and everybody else was very polite about staying out of my way. Telepathy must have wonderful advantages; it also has disadvantages, and the Vesci were just beginning to find that out. I planned to help their education along a little.

And mine, too. I lugged my big girl with the long orange-colored hair out of the car, through the garage entrance into my kitchen, and straight on into the living room. Everybody was busy somewhere else—taking care of Jimmy, I guessed, with a watch set up to dispose of any intruders. I hadn't seen whoever'd been put on watch, but why should I have? They wouldn't be there to bother me.

I dumped the big girl on what I remembered fondly as a fine Chinese white rug (preSpace). Things had happened to it, some of which I have mentioned. I revised my damage estimate upward every time I noticed my house again, and was more and more determined that, by God, Cub IV was going to pay me.

God knows I wasn't about to stand the expense. I'd come there for a vacation, hadn't I?

Well . . . the girl dumped, I let out a yell for Raythorne and/or Liz, if available. My Totum trundled in first. I'd given Liz his controls, I recalled, before leaving for the farm. Now he went on by me and over to the front window—what had been the front window before it had got shot out.

He gave the outside world a good scan, left to right and back, and turned and went out again. As far as he was concerned, I didn't exist.

Silently, I congratulated Liz. A Totum and my couple of Robbies slaved to him made a better watch than any human combination.

But time was passing. The big girl was stirring a bit. I let out another yip.

Liz came clattering down the stairs from what had once been my lovely bedroom.

"Jimmy's coming to," she said. "And he's needed more blood—we're all needed up there. This had better be important, Knave." She was looking at me with a damned stern expression on her face. In another second her hips were going to grow fists.

I gestured at the girl on the floor, now wiggling with some real appearance of consciousness.

Liz gave her a single, brief glance. "All right, who is she? And what makes her important?"

The girl tried to roll over. She said something along the lines of: "Urr," deep in her throat. I sighed and went over and tapped her once more near the back of the head. Peace, perfect peace, with loved ones far away.

"She's our secret weapon," I said.

"Quit being funny," Liz snapped. "We haven't got the time for it."

"I'm not," I said. "This girl is one of the Vesci."

"The what?"

Liz didn't know about the christening. "The aliens," I said. "She's been taken over."

I knew just what Liz was thinking when she shook her head. It went: *Men!* "Half the population has been taken over," she said. "What's so special about her —except for her size and shape?" She gave me a glance intended to wither. "Or is that what you're interested in?" she went on. "If you like them big and solid, I will admit she's attractive. If you're thinking of starting a harem——"

I didn't point out that a harem required more than one female resident, and that the obvious second member—Hell, first member—was right there in the room. I said: "She doesn't act like the others. She acts like a human being."

Liz only said: "So they've managed it," and it was my turn to stare.

"You expected it?"

"Something of the sort," she said. "Obviously, they have a lot of human behavior patterns on tap now—remembered in the minds they've taken over. All they have to do is put that knowledge together, and make it into a set of working instructions—with the particular human mind they use always more or less on tap as a self-correcting feedback. I didn't think it would take them as long as three days."

I said: "But you see what it means, don't you?"

Liz said: "Get her tied up. Thoroughly. Now."

She was right: the big girl was stirring again. Ropes. . . .

I nodded. "If she gets any livelier," I said, "hit her first, and wonder about it afterward."

"What do you think I am?" Liz said. "Naturally. And where will you be?"

"Getting rope."

It turned out to be insulated wire—about half a mile of it for which Harry had not yet found use, lying in a bundle back in the garage. I grabbed it and came on back.

Before I entered the living room I heard voices.

"We are all the same," the big girl was saying, in that imitation-dead tone.

"No, you're not," Liz said. "Some of you have managed to be—well, nearly human beings. We'd like to know why."

"We are all alike," the big girl said.

"You might as well give that up," Liz told her. "You woke up and you tried to kill me and you found out it didn't work. There's no way for you to get away. In a few seconds——"

The conversation wasn't getting anywhere, so I came in. The big girl was sitting on my ex-rug. Liz was standing over her, not too close, with a metal statuette in one hand. The big girl was nursing her own right hand, and I thought I could figure out what had happened while I'd been gone.

"You are now going to be tied up efficiently and

thoroughly," I announced. The girl spun round to stare at me. I could see her muscles tense for a first move.

"And if you try to escape," Liz put in, "Knave is just as fast as I am—and just as powerful."

No time to argue that particular left-handed compliment. I got round behind the girl as she sat, unrelaxed but absolutely still—waiting for her opening. I wasn't about to give her one.

I said: "Liz. To one side."

She stood on the girl's right. I stood behind her to the left. No chance to use her feet. I grabbed an arm.

Strong girl. I could hold it, I could even move it, but it took effort.

Liz grabbed the other arm and hung on.

I said the Hell with it; we weren't Indian-wrestling. I gave her left arm a good yank round. She began to spin with it, but I used my free hand on her shoulder and brought her arm all the way round behind to meet her right one. Liz was still hanging on to that one.

The girl was wriggling. I held her arm with one hand, used the other to try uncoiling some of the damn wire—and then realized what I was doing and said the Hell with it again.

I let go. She spun round, trying to gather her feet under her. I moved into the right position for it and hit the button with my fist.

Peace, perfect peace: why do things the hard way?

"If you keep knocking her out, you'll do some real damage," Liz said.

"Sure," I said, busy with the wire. "In twenty or thirty years I could turn her into a fair facsimile of an old and broken-down boxer. But I don't figure we'll have to keep on that long."

Her arms were now behind her, relaxed. I tied her

ankles together first, then single-looped them to her thighs, and put her down on her side. The wrists and elbows came next, and that was that. The knot for the leg-ties was in front, and her hands were in back. She hadn't shown any signs of being a reincarnation of Houdini.

She did take more time than usual coming out of it. I began to wonder whether Liz, after all, didn't have a point.

But when she did come out she looked as clear-eyed as ever, and she was still going with her imitation. "You cannot keep me long," she said, to me and Liz equally: we were standing in front of her, facing the window from the center of the room.

"We might not have to," I said. "This may not take long."

My Totum went by again, gave the window the same scan, and went out. The girl didn't even follow it with her eyes. She was very good.

"How many like you are there?" Liz said. The obvious first question, and why not?

"We are all the same," the girl said: needle stuck in the groove.

I said: "How many can look human? All of you? Six of you?"

"We are all the same."

"Not all," Liz said, "or you'd all be doing it. We'd have heard about that, and fast. In fact, there can't be any large number like you."

Obvious, but maybe it gave the big girl, and the rest of the Vesci net unavoidably listening in, some notion that we could think. "All right," I said. "How many?"

"We are all——"

And I said, very suddenly: "What's your name?"

She said. "Doris Amble——" before she could catch herself.

"Ambleside," Liz said. "Mother, father, six kids. Father's a Senate official."

All right: I'd heard of him. But I didn't know family status. "How many of your family have—changed?" I said.

She just looked at me. Liz said: "We can find out on the phone."

"So we can." The girl looked stubborn. She'd been wiggling, trying to figure a way out of her ropes, with no success. "Meanwhile, I want to know where the others like her are, right now—and who they are. We're going to have to send out some warnings, at the very least."

My Totum went by again.

"What makes you think she'll tell us?" Liz asked me.

"She'll tell us," I said. "These aliens have things to do—and they're all in the same net. A little pain, administered at unpredictable intervals——"

"We are all the same," the girl said. Back to square one.

"Sure," I told her. "That's what I was getting at."

Then the bomb went off.

XXII

I got my secret weapon into the garage in a hurry; it's the nearest thing to a fireproof structure I own. It's the new concrete-type block; it transmits heat slowly, and it doesn't melt.

The whole house is fireproof, sure—anyhow, it's built out of fireproof imitation wood, like most of the others. But the furnishings aren't.

And the bomb was giving out quite enough heat of its own, right smack outside my living-room window opening.

Transmitted heat: my rug began to smolder, the phono rig, a table, a chair or so . . .

The bomb was a slow, hot burner. Before too long, I knew, the whole inside of the house would be in flames. The shell was fireproof; and what did that matter?

I looked around—and didn't see Liz.

Or anybody else.

There were five people in that house, and one of them, at least, hooked up to enough tubing so that he'd be in trouble if he had to be moved.

I checked the doors. Locked and solid. My big girl—Doris Ambleside that was, so to speak—would be out of harm's way in the garage for a while. But the five people inside . . .

I shut and locked the kitchen door on my way back

in. The door from kitchen to living room was a sheet of flame: matters were progressing damned fast. I remembered that the stairs going up were in the living room.

All in all, it seemed to be Knave-to-a-Crisp Day.

I told myself they might all have got out while I'd been busy with Doris. While I was trying to kid myself with that one, I was heading into the damned flames.

They were too bright. I couldn't see my way . . .

I thumbed a button automatically. It reminded me of the final stupidity I was going to be allowed to make on Cub IV: I had used up my quota in a big fat hurry, and I knew it.

This one was the only one of the bunch that worked in my favor.

I'd forgotten all about my armor. I don't usually wear it in the house, but we'd been busy with Doris, and . . .

Well, it isn't usually a flaming house, either. This was my second for the day, but that didn't make it your usual expectable event.

Even the armor wasn't going to help if I stayed in the house too long. I went through to the staircase, peering through the polarization square. The stairs were more imitation stuff, and they'd hold; likewise the basic floors and walls.

I went up at a dead run, and I met Harry coming down. I bumped into him, as a matter of fact; I was thinking so hard I wasn't doing much looking.

He was babbling at me: "They're all crazy up there! They're trying to get out the windows—"

"They're better off than you are," I said. "The

whole place down there is on fire; where do you think you can get to?''

He goggled. He was in his element—total catastrophe. I suppose he should have been calm and adjusted about it; but somewhere, even in Harry, there must have been a spark of hope—and it was the spark of hope that had turned him into a panic-ridden imbecile.

I said: ''Come with me,'' and went on up. He followed; he had to. You don't give a panicked man any more choices than you have to, and I'd grabbed his wrist and towed him around and up after me.

Upstairs was a milder version of my domestic inferno.

The bedroom hadn't been touched, not quite; fire was creeping along the expensive real wallpaper I'd got for the upstairs halls. I went in to the bedroom dragging Harry.

Liz and Raythorne were preparing to lower Jimmy, complete with tubing and one attached fractionator assembly. They'd rigged a sort of giant sling out of an entire bedsheet—strong enough, and it should have been; it was one of my very best—and gathered it at the top. There they'd tied another sheet as a rope, and were just lifting the whole mess out the window. Tom, I figured, had to be down on the ground waiting to receive the bundle and berth it gently.

It occurred to me that we were not going to be any safer outside. The character who had tossed our little firebomb had no particular reason to go anywhere else, and he could pot any one of us as we came out—if he had a few helpers, and why not, he could cover every door and window.

I must have made some sound. Liz said, without turning: "It's all right. We sent a Robbie out first thing."

I couldn't make sense of that. I said so. Harry moaned and pulled at my hand. Maybe he still thought he could make it, unarmored, down the stairs and through the flames.

Maybe he just wasn't thinking. Some people, I understand, sometimes don't. It's a bad habit to get into. As Liz explained, I began to suspect myself of it, too.

"A Robbie with instructions," she said. "Totally deaf, to begin with. And orders to pay no attention to any messages until its job was complete. It had a machine pistol in its best hand."

"Oh," I said. "With instructions from you to spray the entire surrounding area."

"Twice," Liz said. "All round the house. There ought to be enough room: we won't hit neighbors."

All this time, she and Raythorne were lowering their bundle, steadily and slowly. Liz was taking most of the weight, Raythorne helping with guidance. It looked to me like the sort of trick that would make medical history, if any of us lived.

"The Hell with the neighbors," I said. "Anybody close enough to be hit with a machine pistol is close enough to be on fire."

"Anyhow, he did his job," Liz said, and they reached bottom. She peered down, waited for Tom to settle the bundle and give her safe clearance, and stepped into space.

Behind me, at the doorway, the fire was on its way in. My back felt a trifle warm. Harry must have felt even warmer; he was doing a great deal of moaning. He increased tempo and volume when he saw Liz go out, and then he started toward the window.

Raythorne, meanwhile, peered down, looked all round, and nodded.

You really haven't lived until you've seen a little old lády, looking just like something pressed in lavender for two hundred and forty years, step casually out of a second-story window and vanish.

I let Harry drag me. When we got to the window he stopped as if he'd run into a brick wall. The bedroom was just beginning to go, starting away back at the door. But it would go fast.

While I was silently bidding it a fond farewell, I was thinking. If I went out first, Harry would stand at the window and moan until he was a small crisp corpse.

Besides, I had the armor.

Besides, the captain always goes down with his house—right?

So I picked him up—he was somewhere between Tom and Jimmy for height, and easily Tom's equal for weight—and looked out and down. Tom must have made it alone, and either known how to fall or been plain lucky; from then on, I saw, they'd had a double-sized bedspread out there as a landing-net (except for Jimmy, probably, who'd have been taken by hand), manned by Tom, both Robbies and my Totum.

Okay, everybody was off the net, and it was held right. I swung Harry out into space. He was doing a lot of wiggling and moaning.

"Put me down!" he screamed as he passed the sill. "Knave, you'll get us killed, put me down!"

As ordered.

I put him right into the landing net.

He bounced once, screamed, hit again and began that moan all over, once more. Liz appeared, and helped him slowly off. He sort of fell on his face off the bedspread and landed in my flowers. Up to then, somehow, they hadn't been touched.

Cub IV colonists called them button-downs, I'd never asked why. Big purple blooms like hairy tulips. I'd had a nice bed of them, round that side of the house.

Damn it . . . I took a breath and went out the window. I hit the bedspread with only a small bounce, rolling with it, and got off on the side away from the house.

I did get one look at my carefully cultivated flower bed.

Cub IV, by God, was going to pay, and pay.

Liz was folding the spread. Raythorne was over by Jimmy, on the ground in his sheet. Tom stood there too. The Totum and the two Robbies made a sort of guard around the group.

Harry lay on his face among my flowers.

"Get up," I said, and he got up, slowly and jerkily, looking foolish and a little blank. His face and hands and clothing—all of the visible Harry, in fact—was full of dirt and the remains of hairy tulips.

He didn't say anything. The moan had stopped. Behind us, I could hear my furnishings in flames.

Everybody had turned to me at the sound of my voice—as if they'd all been Robbies or personal Totums.

I sighed. "All right, gang," I said. "What do we do now?"

XXIII

"One good thing," Liz said after a pause. "At least the phone is gone. That cancels your error, Knave. You can't use the phone link."

Liz was a very bright girl. The stunt she'd pulled with my Robbie, deafening it first so it couldn't receive any This-is-contrary-to-the-welfare-of-human-beings orders, was a shining example.

But she'd just made two mistakes. I began to feel a little better.

"The inside phone is melted, sure," I said. "Soft plastics, not like this house stuff. But my personal phone is on the same circuit—right, Harry?"

"Circuit?" he said. He brushed some dirt off his face. It occurred to me that handing Harry a technical question was the fastest way to revive him. A really tough one, some day, might bring him straight out of his coffin. "Your personal phone . . . circuit . . ." He blinked. "Oh. Of course. It's the same circuit. It will work just the same."

And my personal phone was on my belt, where it belonged—neatly protected by my armor. Harry didn't even have to do any more wiring . . .

Then I blinked. It came to me that I'd forgotten something.

"I'll be right back," I said. "Tom?"

He didn't look up.

"Raythorne," I said, "is Tom needed there for the next minute or so? I've got another job for him."

"He won't be needed until we have to decide where to locate Jimmy for good. And even then, Jimmy may not need further blood work." She nudged Tom. He looked down at her, and then over at me.

"Come on," I said. "I've got a lady I want you to help carry."

The garage door was still solid, and still locked. I opened it with the code pulse from my buzzer, and watched it swing out of sight.

She hadn't gone away, and she hadn't been burned or strangled, and she hadn't somehow managed to strangle herself on her wires.

She was just as I'd left her, wrapped and tied, my very own little present.

"Meet Doris," I told Tom. "My secret weapon, I think. Let's get her the Hell out of here."

It took the two of us. How I'd carried the woman alone, I didn't know—same way I'd carried Harry, I suppose. If you have to do it, you can do it. But Doris was a damned heavy girl, and it was pleasant not to have to. I took the knee end, and Tom took the head and shoulders.

She didn't resist at all. Like the other aliens: as soon as they discovered they couldn't get out of whatever tie they were in, they quit struggling. Waste of energy; they figured to save it for more useful things, later.

And there we were, when we'd dumped her, standing around in the open air. Waiting for somebody to come along and try taking us again, by hand, machine or combination.

It struck me that we were not in the best possible position. Liz had removed the immediate threat, but sooner or later somebody would come along. I had a reputation; I'd become, by default more or less, the leader of the human stand on Cub IV: I was a prime target. So, by extension, were the rest of the people I had around me.

It's nice to be famous.

Staying out in the air did not seem like a good idea. Unfortunately, trekking over to a nearby house—or driving to one further away—didn't seem to be a lot better. If we could be burned out of one house, we could be burned out of another, and I didn't want to go through the experience twice.

I had some work to do with my secret weapon, and I had to have a place to do it.

After a second or two, I told everybody to get into the cars—both safe in the garage through everything, like my prize package—and follow me. Only Harry stopped to ask: "Where are we going?"

"Just follow along," I said. He did, in the second car, driven by Liz with her usual aplomb.

And pretty soon we arrived—at, of course, the Government Building.

Solid stone: no burnout. And easily defensible, if we really had to make a stand.

Unless the Vesci had already decided to make a stand there . . .

I told everybody to stay in the cars. I got out all alone, in my armor. Sure enough, a beam lit it up.

So we'd just have to clean them out, I thought. I went back to the car, which was not being fired on—out of good range, and maybe they were a little ammunition-

141

short, or had discovered that my car was hard to dent after their try with the heli.

I got Liz out of the second car, fast, and into the first one, where my secret weapon was bundled up safely next to the driver's seat.

I gave her full instructions.

Then I marched toward the Government Building entrance—that impressive pile of stone with its big fake-marble doors and the unbreakable-plastic stained-glass-type windows—all alone, one man against a horde of enemies, armed only with righteousness, a slug gun, a beamer, and the directions I'd given Liz.

I didn't think I'd have too much trouble.

I wounded three, killed none, which was about the way I wanted it. Two got clean away. I let them go; we needed to get inside more than we needed to run up a record score of Vesci casualties.

Seems they weren't shooting very well. It's hard to pay full attention to your weapon when your nose and your ears are being twisted now and then, hard, at irregular intervals.

That was what I'd told Liz to do with Doris Ambleside; it was the same notion I'd used on the heli pilot. Sooner or later the Vesci were going to come up with a defense against it—though I couldn't imagine one that didn't cut them out of their own network. But pulling it twice didn't seem too pushy.

And it did work—very nicely indeed. A lot of shots burned the air; except for mine, unbothered by distractions, none of them hit anybody.

And when I was sure the place was empty, I invited

the others in. I did tell them to come in fast; there were always neighboring roofs and windows, though the Government Building didn't have very wide alleyways around it—bad city planning, I'd always thought; what you want in an official building is lavish space, inside and out. Gives you the feeling that your money is being spent for something tangible, at the very least—and how much more satisfaction can any government give its citizens?

We located in a courtroom, an inside room without windows, and I locked and bolted the doors —imitation-wood, these were, but thicker than ordinary house doors. The judge's thrones and the attorneys' benches we left alone, as we did the witness box and most of the spectator seating. We grouped in the press section, which was very roomy and had lots of good solid-wood chairs and a couple of strong tables, and I directed Tom and Liz to put my secret weapon down on one of the tables.

The place smelled musty, as if lawbooks had been rotting there for thousands of years. Apparently all courtrooms everywhere smell like that; it must come with the furnishings. The whole damn Government Building, after all, was less than twenty years old.

Doris still didn't struggle. Her orange hair fanned out behind her head as she looked up at me, her eyes open and an expression of calm on her face that made me doubt for a second that anybody had been twisting her nose and ears.

"We are all the same," she told me.

It was a record I remembered hearing. "How many are there like you?"

"We know you're different," Liz said. "And we know there can't be many like you. We can get information from you—and you won't like the methods. You'd better tell us now."

Doris was a little green. Even her orange hair seemed to blanch a trifle. For real bloodthirstiness, give me a practical woman every time; no man can match her, and few have ever tried. Liz's threat had overtones, in that assured voice, of every torture known to man, and a few variations she'd been saving for special occasions. It left no doubt, that tone, that this was such an occasion.

Doris opened her mouth and then shut it again. I think it was the only time I ever saw the Vesci indecisive; perhaps they had never run into anything like Liz before.

I happened to turn—just happened to.

Jimmy was on the other table, Raythorne fussing over him. She didn't look frighteningly concerned, so I thought probably all was going to be well. Harry was sitting in a wooden chair, watching everything with a certain gloomy interest. He'd fully recovered from the burning house, not to mention his adventures among my flowers; he was quite his usual mournful self, expecting no good of anybody or anything.

And Tom was . . .

Oh, Hell. Tom looked as green as Doris did. He was shivering, in a fine tremble I had never seen in him before.

Doris was shivering, too, as much as her ropes would allow.

"All right," I said, "I know where one other like you is. Now where are the rest?"

XXIV

It was wrong; it was all wrong.

Tom couldn't be one of them. Tom had to be immune.

I knew that. I was certain of it. But he stood there, and whatever I knew went out the window.

They were not stupid. Doris made a move toward rolling off the table at the same second Tom made his break for the door, far behind us at the end of the spectator seating.

I didn't watch Doris. Tom went down with a slug in his shoulder, and didn't get up.

Raythorne was at his side instantly. I shooed her away while we got him tied, foot-hobbles at least and his hands loosely wired across his chest. Then she took over.

It struck me that Raythorne, and the rest of the human hospital staff, were all in for a rush of business—it had already started, and it was going to go on long after the small war we'd walked into was over.

I didn't want to talk to Tom. That had been one fine imitation, down to his black looks about Tobor. When he knew all the time what had happened to Tobor. . . .

And when Tom, I realized, had set me up for those shots going across the damn plank into Central Exchange.

Sure, he'd had an answer. And it had been plausible, almost as plausible as his act. But it had bothered me at the time; I remembered filing it.

I took it out of file and burned it. I had my answer; I knew who had tipped the guards we were coming. I didn't want it—I wished I'd never heard of it—but I had it.

I had a small pile of questions, too, since Tom had been handed any number of opportunities to pot me since the very beginning. But the Vesci were intelligent—belt *and* suspenders. Tom was the belt.

Call it not letting your left hand know what your right hand is doing. That's not possible for a human being, and it's not possible for a single telepathic network like the Vesci plus ex-humans; but if you work at it you can manage a good imitation of it. Rub your head and pat your belly—that sort of thing. Or play two whole different tunes on one piano, one hand per tune.

The main tune was the war. But the Vesci were smart enough to have a second tune. It was a Hell of a compliment, when I thought about it later.

I was a survival expert. I had a reputation for knowing all sorts of things that might help a race survive, and many handy facts of all sorts. And the Vesci knew at once that some humans were resistant—that they couldn't take us all in and wipe out the colony. So they started the war.

At the same time—second tune—they set an eye on me. How do I do what I do? What brand of decision do I make? In what new ways (new both to Vesci and to human experience as far as they knew it) did I respond?

The war had involved several earnest efforts to kill

me, and might involve more. But—until Tom was wrapped and tied—it had also involved that eye. The left hand, doing something entirely different, and never directed to stop. Maybe, just maybe, I would provide some little hint that would show up a fatal weakness in the human race.

Or—just as likely—I'd show the Vesci how to use any number of new survival tricks—against humanity.

It made sense. It fit.

I hated it.

Liz had effectively blocked Doris back onto the table by then, with a little help from Harry. I went there, leaving Tom in the aisle between spectator seats, with Raythorne at work on him.

He'd given Jimmy his blood. Did that mean that Jimmy . . .

No: telepathy was mind-connected, not body-connected. Or the Vesci could have had us all, even in the hospital, with a few simple swipes of the scalpel.

Jimmy was safe.

But Tom—Tom shouldn't have been one of them. It was all wrong.

It was . . . well, of course it was wrong. Because he'd been acting.

You might say that a large light went on over my head. You might say I had a vision.

You might say I finally got in touch with the back of my head. If Tom had been acting all along . . .

Then the act was what had prevented me from seeing the answer. I knew what made people immune. Just one thing, one little thing; and it explained everything. More staff than patients and visitors immune at the hospital? Sure. My group immune? Harry was a problem, but not for long; if I could be immune, and bloodthirsty Liz, then Harry could qualify, too.

Doris said: "We will not tell you of anything."

"Go ahead," I said. "Don't tell."

Liz looked at me.

"What's going on?" I said. "Has anybody been in touch with the rest of the world?"

The rest of Cub IV was pretty messy.

Fighting was continuing, hand-to-hand, in half the streets of the city—we were lucky we hadn't run into anything on the way to our station. Liz had been pulling reports in from my phone—which she'd taken, with my permission, when we came into the courtroom; at the time she'd wanted the survey more than I did.

Now I wanted it more.

The outlying farms and houses outside the city . . . some were peaceful now, and some were just silent. It depended on who had won out; if humans had come through, they were peaceful.

But the Vesci didn't mind killing humans not in their network. Of course not: they had no empathy with the rest of us, with individuals who couldn't share their mind.

Can a telepathic race ever develop empathy?

I'd asked the question—how long before? Now I had the answer: no. And I knew what the question meant.

"We've got to do something," Liz said. "This is a bloodbath. The world is dying—people are being killed—Knave, you can't just stand there and let this go on while you satisfy your curiosity, or make some grandiose plan——"

"I don't intend to let it go on," I said. Make that two big lights over my head, or two visions.

Though the second one was not exactly new. It was, more or less, what I'd meant when I'd told Liz that the phone link was no disadvantage.

"Then what are you going to——"

I took the phone back from her.

"I'm going to broadcast," I said. "Harry?"

He blinked. "What is it, Knave?" His tone implied that I was about to ask him to commit obscene acts in public.

"Can you rig a loudspeaker from here? My link will reach anybody at home, but it won't reach the people in the streets. And I'll have to reach them too. I'll have to reach everybody."

"There's a loudspeaker setup upstairs," he said. "If you want me to bring the mikes and leads down here——"

I looked at Tom and at Doris Ambleside.

Both seemed in good hands, and not likely to cause any serious trouble.

"No need to bother," I said. "Can that rig be heard all over the city?"

Harry pondered for a second. "It probably can, if I beef up the circuits a little," he said. "What I mean to do——" He hesitated. "On the other hand, there might be difficulties. Unless the circuit is the usual double AR 75——"

He was back to normal. "Let me know about difficulties when, as, and if they happen," I said. "Meanwhile, let's go. I'll leave our prisoners here for the time being. You can beef up the loudspeaker, and I'll get my phone, and I'll talk to everybody."

"But, Knave," Liz asked me. "What are you going to *say*?"

I gave her a gentle, casual smile. "Wait and find out," I told her. "Everybody is going to know in a very few minutes. You, too."

She looked exasperated. Harry and I headed for the door and on upstairs.

XXV

Upstairs was a small room with a mike stand in it, and a large glassed-in control-room setup hanging over it. There was also a clock on the wall, and a sort of large closet, with lights over the doors, just under the control room. The whole place was imitation stuff, and the floor was a pleasant pattern of squares and lines, if you like that sort of thing. I felt as if I were standing in the middle of a wiring diagram for a Highland kilt with communicator arrangements.

Harry looked around, said: "Hm," shut the door behind us, and disappeared into the large closet. I stood around in front of the mike, wondering what the Hell was going on all over the planet. People were fighting and dying. The alien masquerade certainly continued, and a human being here and there was being struck down by someone he thought of as his best friend, his wife (or her husband), his child—you name it.

A lovely picture. I tried not to think about it. This was going to be my big move; I had to stay calm.

I don't know how much time passed. A lot less than I

thought. Then Harry suddenly popped up in the control room—apparently that closet had a set of stairs in it, or a ladder—and waved at me. He said something.

He was totally inaudible. I waved back.

He said something else. He made gestures. They were very expressive gestures, but I didn't know what they were trying to express.

I made some gestures, too. Hands spread wide. Wrinkled puzzlement on noble brow. Appeal for help in raised eyebrows.

He got the idea. I could see him get it; he mouthed: "Oh," which I could lip-read without trouble, and raised one finger.

Wait one something, obviously. Hour? Minute? Second?

Less than a minute, more than a second. His voice came booming out into my small room with the effect of God handing down the rule-book for mankind.

"Sorry about that," God said. "Forgot we were switched off up here."

Engineers do have a tendency that way—the royal "we," I mean. Most control-room engineers have the strong belief that they run the lives of the people out in the studio. The trouble with that belief is that it is, to a certain small extent, true.

And Harry was being a control-room engineer. In his element.

"Now we're switched on," I said, into the mike. "What do I——"

"You don't have to talk into that," Harry said. "Not to me. That's just the loudspeaker hookup. Let me know when you're ready and I'll cut you in."

"Okay," I said, in Harry's general direction. "I'm

going to want this to go out on loudspeaker and phone both, so I'll make the general phone-link call and then talk into my phone and the speaker, both. All right?"

"What about feedback?" Harry said.

"I don't know," I said patiently. "What about it?"

He thought for a second. Anyhow, he pursed his lips and wrinkled his forehead. "I know how we can work it," he said. "Can you detach your phone?"

"Sure."

"Then detach it and give it to me. I'll take it up here." Now and then he was just Harry, for brief seconds; then he became We again. "We'll hook it up to a control-room auxiliary speaker—so the phone will be picking up just what goes out over the speakers. No double-miking, no feedback; we can manage it."

"Great," I said.

For one second I stood, frozen.

Tom had been acting, and had fooled me.

If Harry were acting, too. . . .

No. If Harry had been acting, or Liz, or Raythorne, they'd never have helped me rig the phone link, or got us all out of the burning house, or . . .

They were safe; they were human. The Vesci had needed only one spy.

Harry had disappeared again. The door of the closet opened and he came toward me with his hand out.

I fiddled with the connections and unclipped my phone and handed the thing to him. "Take good care of it," I said. "It's the only one I have left."

"You know," Harry said casually, "a heli could probably lay a bomb right on top of this building, and wipe us all out."

"If he had a big enough bomb. Which he doesn't—whoever's in that heli—because big, dependable bombs take time to build, and there weren't any ready-made. Not on Cub IV, not after twenty years of peace and quiet."

"Still . . ." Harry sighed.

I waved him back. "Okay, it's possible," I said. "If it makes you feel any better, we could all be dead in the next ten seconds. Now get back to home base."

He went into the closet.

I'd been accurate: the thing I'd given Harry was my only phone. But it was not my only communicator.

A space-four channel straight back to the Comity worlds, ready to be piped into any handy starship, was what I'd been holding back. As I say, I do draw some weight. Not enough to call for a fleet to evacuate all of humanity from the planet. Enough, I was fairly sure, for one ship, and one specified duty.

And one carefully chosen crew and captain, too.

I cupped my mouth with my hand, and I talked straight into the communicator; it doesn't even look like a phone, it's a flat plate maybe three inches square, and I usually wear it along one hip, far enough forward so it doesn't stab me when I sit down, far enough back so it doesn't stab me when I walk either.

Harry was waiting, up there. I had to take a few minutes—and it had to be in as solitary a spot as I could get. That room looked like my best chance.

I got through fairly fast—individual space-four communicators are by no means standard-issue equipment for civilians, and when a civilian suddenly starts a call on one he is likely to get a great deal of instant attention—and I made my requests. I had to go over the whole thing a couple of times, in varying degrees of detail.

People kept saying: "But that's impossible!" when I told them about the Vesci.

Very well, it was impossible. But it was happening. And the actual things that happen don't care in the slightest what you call them, impossible or weird or green cheese—I finally made that point. From there on it was fairly simple.

And it didn't really take too long; three minutes, maybe. At most, four. Harry kept looking up, apparently waiting for the bomb that wasn't going to happen.

We were all through with bombs—mostly.

I cut out of circuit and tucked the flat plate away, and took a deep breath. Harry was still staring straight up.

"Harry."

"What?" he said. His head came back to normal position. "Oh. You're ready now?"

"I'm ready now," I said.

"I'll make the call. I think everybody within reach of a phone will pick up on us."

"They ought to; I've been the main broadcast link since all this started." I waited while Harry punched in his code, and phones all over Cub IV's city and country human habitations began to ring and buzz and flash.

Another minute, maybe. Then he looked at me. "Okay, Knave," he said. "You're on."

I took another deep breath.

"This is a final notice, not a drill," I said. "I'm talking to everybody I can reach—every human being, every alien. I want you all to hear this one.

"Many of you know me, or know my reputation. You know I can get things done—some very big things done, when they're needed. And they're needed now. We've been in a war, and there's been a lot of bloodshed. That war has to be stopped.

"All right: it's stopped.

"I have notified Comity starships that the entire human population of this planet is to be picked up and resettled elsewhere. There are other new worlds open; you won't be going to any world already settled." That was to remove temptation from the imitation-humans in the listening crowd. "Besides, no alien would be able to stand a long space trip; the distance would cut him off from the network here. I don't think that's a pleasant prospect.

"Nor is it a necessary one. The human beings will be leaving this planet. At 1300 hours tomorrow, every human being within sound of my voice—and every other one you can find and inform—should be at the landing-field—the original colonist's landing field.

"Arrangements have been made to pick you up there. Humanity will stop this war—by leaving Cub IV alone.

"I am authorized to make my statement an instruction, with the full power of the Comity backing it.

"Every human being is to be at the landing field at 1300 hours tomorrow. There are no exceptions. There should be no delays.

"And you others—you non-human beings within sound of my voice—know now that further fighting is unnecessary. All you have to do is to wait until 1300 hours tomorrow afternoon. At that time we will all be at the field, and you will be—on this planet, alone.

155

"I suggest that you return any human beings under your control, if you can. I can't give you orders. But any human being not at that field at that time will be presumed to be taken over by aliens—no matter whether or not he acts like it. Some of them, as you may have found out, don't.

"I can't instruct the aliens. I am not trying. But I am instructing the human beings.

"Be at the field. Be there on time. All of you. This is an order—direct from the Comity."

I switched off.

I signalled Harry to cut the loudspeaker link. He did something in the control room, and nodded back at me. I was off the air.

It would work: I had a reputation to trade on, and orders from the Comity were not to be fooled with. The human beings would be at the field, as specified.

Most of them, anyhow.

I waited for Harry, and took my phone back. I made a couple of fast, individual calls to places I knew were safe.

Then I went down to the courtroom again.

Tom and Doris were still tied. It was Tom who opened his eyes and looked at me.

"There will be no more fighting," he said.

I looked back. "Somehow," I said, "I don't want to hear it from you. I don't want to hear anything from you. I know you're all the same, with the same message——"

"There will be no more fighting," Doris chipped in. Natural voice, no trace of the alien monotone.

The masquerade, as far as these two were concerned, was over. I had a few minutes to indulge curiosity in: "Tell me something," I said to her. "How is it that some of you can retain human characteristics—or fake them—and most can't?"

"We do not know," Doris said. "Some few—those whose minds are most resistant, among the many we have added to our network; the few we very nearly could not touch at all—retain individual habit patterns of speech and motion. As we learned this, we were able to use it, or suppress it—whichever seemed best tactically at the time."

My eyebrows went up. "What do you people—you things—know about tactics? What you've picked up from us?"

"You are not the first race we have met," Doris said. As I listened, I thought I could catch a faint alien undertone in her voice, a sort of accent.

Maybe it had been in Tom's voice, too, right along. I didn't know, or want to know.

"What happened to the others?"

"They were not resistant," Doris said. "We have never found a resistant race before."

I got quite a lecture on Vesci history. What I learned, I used to start this report with.

After a while, I wasn't interested any more. I was just—sick.

Human beings have a bloodier history. But there is something about the idea of mental control . . .

Maybe it's just me. Anyhow, I said: "All right. Let's go home."

Raythorne looked up from tending Jimmy. "We can

move him just like Tom, now," she said calmly. "He doesn't need special support. He'll be conscious in an hour, perhaps less."

"Fine," I said. "Let's get going."

Somehow, we spent the time until 1300 hours the next afternoon. There wasn't much to do, but we ate and slept—crowded into Liz's small box of a house, which hadn't been burned out. I did my best with the materials at hand, but I doubt I turned out anything fit for writing down or remembering; Liz was, and is, beautiful, sane and competent, but she's not much of a cook and she doesn't keep much in store.

Well, it was something to do. I did it.

XXVI

I also found opportunities to talk to Liz, to Raythorne and even to Jimmy. Hell, I even talked to Harry.

One at a time, casual, private. Doris and Tom were still with us, which was the way I wanted it; they didn't see anything out of the ordinary. Naturally, they wouldn't be going to the field, unless the Vesci dropped control—and I didn't really think they would. I thought, without too much data, that any mind the Vesci had once owned was theirs for keeps, spoiled for any other use.

As it turned out, I was right. We'd had to be cautious; we'd had to hope for the return of so many human beings . . .

Hope again. They tell me it's a virtue. God knows it makes enough trouble to be a virtue.

And by 1300 hours, the next afternoon, the entire human population of Cub IV was at that field.

The most common single sentence I heard was: "We'll be back."

I'd told the Vesci: we were human beings. We didn't like being kicked off real estate we'd settled.

And we weren't about to be.

I mingled with the field crowds for a bit; they started assembling before noon and I had some time to walk back and forth and eavesdrop. I kept hearing that same thing:

"We'll be back."

And at 1300 hours, they were all at the field—every last one—waiting.

All, of course, except for us.

Liz, Raythorne, Harry, about half of the hospital's human staff, a few others I'd handpicked . . .

Jimmy had wanted to come along. Raythorne had to tell him very authoritatively that he was in no condition to move around. He said he felt fine. She said she was sure he would feel fine, if he stayed flat on his back for a few days.

I sided with Raythorne.

And at about 1301, we started out.

Large bombs are difficult and time-consuming to make, not to mention tricky; most of the stuff you can make large-scale explosives out of has the interesting habit of going off in your hands if you cough the wrong way, or something of the sort.

But great stores of simple gases can be made in

almost no time at all. And we'd had the perfect head-quarters for that: we'd had the hospital, where only human staff was allowed to move freely. Such aliens as there were inside the hospital were tied down the way Jimmy had been—tubing and all the rest; they were injuries the staff had been trying to treat.

I wondered about imitation-humans, but Raythorne and one of the staff doctors had shelved that question.

"We don't need a large crew for this work," the staff doctor had said. "And we can pick just the ones we do need—the ones we have absolutely no doubts about."

Since I knew what made for immunity—and what, in smaller quantities, made for resistance—I could see how the picking was going to be done. And it did look all right.

Unless some imitation stumbled into the working labs . . .

"Nobody will stumble into the working labs," Raythorne told me. "We've fixed that up nicely. It seems one of the staff members has come down with a very painful and highly communicable disease. He's in a whole wing by himself, sealed off—in fact, a small department at the hospital is drawing up special plans to get him off-planet with the rest of us, without risking contagion, when the starships arrive."

Very neat: I wished I'd thought of it myself.

By 1300, we had our materials, and by 1301 we were on the way to the hospital to collect them—by car, heli, anything that moved.

It was a lovely gas, a descendant of the preSpace anaesthetics like cyclopropane. Its aftereffects were mild—a few people would throw up, a few feel dizzy for a while—an hour or so, not more. And it acted a good deal faster than cyclopropane did, and over a much wider area; you could drop it like tear gas, and watch it spread for almost a mile in any direction.

We had the attack planned: we made a lot of overlapping circles of one-mile radius (a little under a mile, actually; we played it as safe as possible, all the way), and we covered the whole of the city and country, anywhere Cub IV colonists had lived, and anywhere they might have got to.

We didn't cover the swamps. Nobody had the slightest idea what the gas would do to Vesci metabolisms; and it wasn't really important, in any case.

Without humans to do their work, the Vesci were out of the running.

And the humans had human metabolisms. They were dropping like flies, all over the inhabited area of the planet.

We didn't run into any opposition at all for the first half-hour. Then, as the aliens began to collect their wits, a few humans we hadn't reached got to helis of their own and set out to try to do something about us.

Helis don't come equipped with weapons—not on Cub IV. But a pilot can carry a beamer, or a slug gun—and it's a fairly stable platform to shoot from.

But we knew which planes were ours, and where each one was supposed to be at a given time.

Strangers blundering into our areas never got a chance to fire. We fired first.

A crashlanded heli may not kill, or even seriously damage, its pilot. We were aiming for the rotors wherever possible.

Damn it, we did *not* want to kill anybody. Where was the sense in that?

But I think three imitation-humans, three who'd been taken over and were flying helis to stop us, did die before we were through. There was no way in the world to avoid that.

I wish there had been. I kept remembering Rame Janssen, the only one I'd killed personally. Maybe one of the few aliens who had died in our small war.

I didn't like to think about him. Or the three in the helis. Or the others I'd had no hand in at all, the ones who had died in one fight or another as humans and aliens chose sides and began to slug it out . . . .

By 1350, thereabouts, we had the situation nicely in command.

Harry went into operation then—Harry and, because it was a job he could do, Jimmy.

Harry had a hand speaker rig—a sort of extra-super-power loud-hailer—which he'd put together out of God knows what in the Government Building—old bits of string and spit, for all I knew. He'd been riding as passenger in one plane, and when that plane was finished its assigned path, it swung away and headed for the field.

I wasn't in it. I was busy in another plane.

But I kept wondering. If, for some mad reason, imitation humans had decided to go along to the field, come with the ordinary humans and wait there to be taken off the planet . . .

By the time Harry got there, they'd know what had happened; they'd know that all their fellows were unconscious.

And they'd try fighting back. There was no other move for them to make, hopeless or not. If they went offworld, they were out of the net—so going with the human beings on the starships made no sense. If they stayed on, they had to do battle with us, at terrific odds; and in order to get any chance at all, they had to start fast. They had to get away from the field crowd, get back to where they could find weapons, where they could oppose us, before our job was done—they had to get the jump on us, if they could.

If they'd come to the field at all . . .

I'd have been sweating small drops of actual blood by the time I got to the field, if I were Harry. Harry tells me he wasn't worrying about a thing; "After all," he says, "what's the worst that could happen?"

With a man like Harry, that is not a question you answer.

And, in any case, it didn't happen.

Harry got to the field while the rest of us were wrapping up Stage Two of our work—landing, and making gift packages out of every unconscious human form we saw.

That was time-consuming.

But I was familiar with ropes and knots. Doctors are just as familiar, if not more so—it goes with the trade. We had a great deal of rope—mostly hospital supplies of various kinds, from the actual ropes used to suspend weights from in fracture cases and the like, to great rolls of bandaging wound and tightened to serve, to a selection of torn bedsheets.

Anything and everything—it wasn't a very neat job, but we didn't want a prize for neatness. We just wanted to get it done, and get it done fast.

Grab—arrange—tie—test your knots. Grab the next one—arrange him—tie—test your knots.

And the next one, and the next . . .

If Cub IV had been settled much longer than twenty years, we'd still be at that job.

As it was, we were through just after sundown.

We even had a few strips of bedsheet left over.

Undoubtedly, we'd missed one or two. But we hadn't missed many—we were careful, and between us we knew almost everyone on the planet. One or two left running around weren't going to be much of a threat.

By then, I hoped, Harry had set up his speakers, and Jimmy had been explaining things to the crowd of human beings—real human beings—at the field.

All we had to do was fly over there, land, and wrap matters up.

The war was over.

The explanations had begun.

XXVII

By the time I got to the field—along with the rest of our little gas-and-tie contingent—the crowd had heard Jimmy's explanations.

Harry's loud-hailer-plus had worked very well. And Jimmy, flat on his back, had managed to make everything very clear—or so I gather, at any rate, from what he told me later. He hadn't done a thing wrong, and he hadn't neglected anything.

The only trouble had been that nobody believed him.

Nobody disbelieved him, either—not exactly. The ships hadn't landed, the sun had gone down and the immense landing field was getting damned chilly with a wind sweeping across it; and the colonists were just standing there, patiently.

Waiting, naturally. Just waiting.

Gerald Knave had got them into their situation; Gerald Knave was going to tell them what the situation really was. They wouldn't settle for substitutes, no matter how well vouched for.

A small percentage of them—small, when you consider the events of the preceding few days—were wounded. Those, like Jimmy, were being kept warm in blankets, tended to by nurses or family members or just friends, sometimes being fed coffee or something stronger.

They weren't making much noise. There was a little muttering as we landed, and came over across the field toward them in a body—I wasn't instantly visible in the gloom, and there were a lot of people who knew Knave, so to speak, but had never met Gerald—people who were familiar with the reputation, but had no idea what the face looked like that went with it.

The sentence I'd been hearing so much before we set out didn't seem to be part of the mutterings now. Whether they fully believed Jimmy or not, the absence of starship passenger boats on the field made his story a little credible.

They weren't saying, now: "We'll be back."

They knew they weren't going to leave.

The muttering grew in volume as we got closer, and by the time we reached the big crowd I was the center of attention. I looked for Jimmy and found him in the front lines, on a stretcher, with Harry's loudspeaker arrangement mostly on his chest, though a few wires or bits of string or something trailed off toward the ground.

Jimmy was blanketed; in fact, he was dozing. For a casualty in only fair shape, he'd had one Hell of a busy day. I looked round, saw Harry standing near, pointed to the electronic wizardry and made a question with my eyebrows.

He nodded.

I picked up the speaker without waking Jimmy. I thumbed it on; the noise was maybe a little less likely to wake him if I stood right next to him where he'd get my voice direct, not amplified . . . but if he woke, he woke; later, he'd be able to sleep in peace.

Later, I told myself, we all would.

The first thing I told the crowd was that they could go home. The starships that were supposed to be coming along to evacuate them would not be coming—had never been planned for.

"The human colony on this planet is safe," I said. "And it is permanent. We're going to stay."

That much brought cheers.

"But there are some jobs to do," I said. "And there are going to be more jobs in the future. Cub IV isn't the planet without a problem any more, and it never will be again.

"The aliens—the Vesci, I call them, and they might as well have a name—the Vesci are going to be here, too. They are not going to be able to take over your minds—and they are not going to be able to get into the minds of any future colonist on Cub IV. But humans and Vesci aren't the only life on this world."

Somebody said: "Animals."

"Right," I told him, and the crowd. "Animals. The ones native to this world—the ones the Vesci almost certainly can control. They may be attacking settlements, isolated houses, anything—and you'll have to remember that you'll be dealing with an animal under intelligent direction. The Vesci may want peace—and I like the idea myself; but if they decide to make a second try at driving us off Cub IV they'll make it with the animals."

"Hell," somebody's bass voice said, "we can take care of that."

"Sure you can," I said. "But you may have to—you won't be the world without problems any more. You'll have to fight, maybe—but if you have to, you can.

"There's another job, though, that's urgent. It has to be done now tonight by a great many of you." I paused and looked around. The crowd was human, and I knew it; and I hadn't realized how much I'd needed to be surrounded by human beings.

I like working alone. I even like living alone, which is one Hell of a rare taste.

(And, as I mentioned, contra-survival, damn it.)

But I'm human, and any human being needs human beings. It's just not something you think of until you're up against things that look human, and aren't.

I felt a great relief, and a great peace.

I also felt damn cold. No reason to stand out in the wind any longer than I had to.

"Some of the telepaths—the native race—took over human minds," I said. "They didn't take over your minds. None of you are alien; all of the aliens have been taken care of.

"They're unconscious—or they are right now. By

the time you get to them they may be coming out of it. And you'll have to go and get them, and bring them here to the field.

"You see, there *will* be a ship landing."

Stirs and mutters. Jimmy had told them the same thing. But Jimmy wasn't Gerald Knave. A reputation is an interesting thing to own.

"That ship—only one, because only one is needed; that's all the room its passengers will take up—is going to take the humans whose minds have been robbed from them off this planet. The humans who have been taken over will leave, just as soon as they can all be brought here, and as soon after that as a passenger boat or two can load them.

"Many of them will be where you expect them to be—where you left them when you came out here. Others will be in houses, in fields—scattered all over. We've got locations for them all; we've done a little bunching together where we could.

"And they're all neatly roped. They won't be any trouble. They can't fight back.

"All you have to do is go and get them and bring them back here. Then they'll be taken off the planet, and only you—humans proven immune to the Vesci, humans who can't be taken over—will remain. And only humans who can't be taken over will come here as Colonists—or come here in the starship and its passenger boats that are due in less than an hour."

More stirs.

"Go and get them," I said. "Ask us for directions, when and if you need them. Take your cars, helis, anything at all; just make sure you gather them all up and bring them back here.

"We'll be waiting, along with the passenger boats."

The crowd began to move. I'd given them a deadline, which is always a good idea—actually, they had nearer three hours than one, and they were going to need it; there was a lot of transporting to be done—and they were off for Operation Cleanup.

I waited, with a few others, on the empty field. The wind didn't get any warmer.

XXVIII

The ship sent down its boats, and the trussed passengers were loaded aboard. Upstairs, they'd be kept in well-guarded quarters; and, as the starship left Cub IV behind, we'd discover whether or not the colonists got their own minds back.

The distance turned out to be something on the order of one hundred million miles—just over one Astronomical Unit. Harry is one of a large crowd of people who are working on that fact, along with everything else learned from and on Cub IV, trying to make sense out of telepathy—and maybe give it to the human race.

I don't think they'll succeed. Not the last bit, at any rate.

For one thing: the humans who'd been taken over lost their Vesci minds about one A. U. out—a little more. But they didn't get their own minds back as replacements.

They didn't get any minds back at all. Not as far as anybody has ever been able to tell.

That was our real casualty list: one starship cargo of human vegetables.

And that was what almost sparked off the Cub IV riot. I didn't hold them down when that time came; I was off the planet by then. I understand Liz did a Hell of a job, and Raythorne, and several good people I didn't happen to run into.

The human beings wanted to rush out and find the Vesci—the real ones—if they had to comb every square inch of planet to do it. They wanted to exterminate the damned clams.

It was a matter of revenge. And revenge is not a motive; it's a disease.

A common disease, sure; so how does that improve it?

The colony got sense talked back into it. As I say, Liz and Raythorne were among the sense-talkers.

It's a very sensible colony, in fact. In one very important way, it may be the best colony humanity has ever planted, anywhere.

Because every member of it—the survivors, and the new colonists who've come on since—has been tested for one quality. The quality that makes for immunity to the Vesci; the quality that means you are not a telepath, and can't be made into one—maybe, it occurs to me, because you don't need to be.

It was waving in my face from the day the whole mess began, but it took me most of our small war to figure it out. The quality most doctors and hospital staff do seem to have—the quality that made me think Tom could not be an imitation . . .

Empathy, it's called.

170

The Vesci had run into one colonizing race before us. That race, as described by the Vesci during my history lesson, doesn't seem to have had anything resembling empathy.

The ability to feel what somebody else feels.

The ability to sympathize—fully, helpfully, regardless of your own needs and troubles.

That's what empathy is, at peak. Luckily, immunity comes a long way before peak, or most of us would be Vesci by now.

But empathy is the quality a telepathic race can't have. It's the thing in our minds the Vesci can't handle, because they aren't equipped to understand it.

Can a telepathic race develop empathy?

With what? Its whole experience has been with itself, and anything it meets becomes either part of itself or dead very shortly.

It's a single being, and it remains a single being no matter how many individual units make it up. "Self-centered" is altogether too weak a word to describe the result; human beings don't have a word for that result, because they've never had that sort of totally lonely, entirely single, experience.

Empathy, it just doesn't have. And can't understand, or deal with, or control.

The ability to feel for and with other human beings . . .

Well, all right: how do you test for it?

There are a lot of rough everyday tests already. You know one or two, maybe more; you use them on the people you meet and the people you associate with.

That was the sort of thing that got used on the captain

and crew of the ship and passenger boats that had to take away our casualties . . . our losses.

The ones you're *sure* have empathy—the ones you'd point out to other people as examples.

Later on, of course, the professionals got into the act.

Psychological testing. They tell me it's a science, now, and it may be; I won't get into the argument. And the tests don't seem to do any harm.

The Cub IV colony is getting along fairly well.

At the moment, it's even getting along peacefully.

The Vesci can't wipe out humanity; and human beings—once an attack of that disease, revenge, is over—don't want to wipe out an intelligent race. (That's empathy, too.)

Maybe the two races can learn from each other. At the moment, that is the way the talk is going.

But I doubt it.

Sooner or later, one race is going to inhabit Cub IV, whether we like it or not. The Vesci don't want to teach us anything, and they've learned about all they're going to learn—from the minds they took over. Any human being who wanted to teach them any skill that gave them more power over their environment would be carefully led away and put somewhere safe and padded.

That environment includes human beings.

No: the Vesci are odds-on to start it, but one way or another there is going to be a final war on Cub IV, one of these centuries.

And human beings, empathetic or not, are odds-on to win that war. It's something they're good at: surviving.

I ought to know.

It's my specialty.

FRITZ LEIBER

*04594 **Babel 17** Delany $1.50

*05476 **Best Science Fiction of the Year** Del Rey $1.25

06218 **The Big Time** Leiber $1.25

*10623 **City** Simak $1.75

16649 **The Dragon Masters** Vance $1.50

16704 **Dream Master** Zelazny $1.50

19683 **The Einstein Intersection** Delany $1.50

24903 **Four For Tomorrow** Zelazny $1.50

47071 **The Last Castle** Vance 95¢

47803 **Left Hand of Darkness** Leguin $1.95

72784 **Rite of Passage** Panshin $1.50

79173 **Swords and Deviltry** Leiber $1.50

80694 **This Immortal** Zelazny $1.50

Available wherever paperbacks are sold or use this coupon.

ace books, (Dept. MM) Box 576, Times Square Station
New York, N.Y. 10036
Please send me titles checked above.

I enclose $................. Add 35c handling fee per copy.

Name ....

Address ....

City..................... State............. Zip........

SCIENCE FICTION from the GREAT YEARS

There are a lot more
where this one came from!